Aki and the Spheres of Time
The Crystal of Yggdrasil

Translation by Maria Bullard

ISBN | 978-88-93217-85-9

The Crystal of Yggdrasil. Aki and the Spheres of Time
Gianni Perticaroli

Illustrations and cover by Luca Rovelli
Translation by Maria Bullard

Gianni Perticaroli

Aki and the Spheres of Time
The Crystal of Yggdrasil

ZERO
A Word of Advice

My name is Achille Chiorri, I'm twelve years old and I wasn't very good at composition in school, so I never would have thought I'd be capable of writing anything much longer than a couple of pages without having a total brain meltdown.

And write a novel? No way!

But here I am, my fingers whizzing over the keyboard, churning out pages and pages about all the things that have happened to me, and the amazing adventures I've had.

Really, it's true.

I imagine some of you are rolling your eyes, wondering what sort of incredible adventures I could have had, seeing I'm just a normal twelve-year-old kid from a small town in Italy that hardly anybody has heard of.

But that's the whole point.

You see, I had always thought I was a normal kid, too, no different from anyone else; but I found out I wasn't. Honestly, I'm not bragging; I'm an Heir to the Superior Beings. There, I said it; and I bet many of you are asking yourselves: "An Heir of what?"

Yes, I know. That was my first reaction, too, when I found out.

However, don't ask me to explain in a couple of sentences what it's about because it's too complicated, so you'll have to continue reading if you want to know more.

And believe me, you should keep reading or you'll miss out on the opportunity of losing yourself in some captivating stories and totally awesome adventures.

Of course, you could also end up deciding that nothing of what you're reading is true, that I made it all up... In other words, that everything I wrote is a lot of baloney.

And I wouldn't blame you if you did.

If I were in your shoes, I would probably feel that way, too.

But believe me, it's not like that at all.

Seriously, all this stuff I'm going to tell you about? It really

happened. And it might get really crazy so just try to stick with it, because who knows what the future has in store for us. You could end up in dangerous and terrifying situations like the ones I found myself in and maybe some of the things I write about will help you.

I hope it never happens, but one day you might kick yourself for not believing me.

ONE
About Me

Usually, I eat breakfast on my own, but that day my little sister Aurora was already up, sullenly dunking cookies in her milk while watching cartoons on TV.

Aurora didn't answer when I wished her good morning, like she didn't even hear me.

I sat across the table from her and added some cereal to the bowl of chocolate milk my mom had set out for me.

"What are you doing up so early?" I asked my sister, who was usually sleeping like a rock at seven in the morning.

"Because you're taking her to school today," answered mom as she walked into the kitchen.

My mom's name is Virginia. She was all dressed up and wearing makeup, too.

I hadn't seen her dressed like that in ages. I also realized that she must have been to the hairdresser's because her brown hair was now glowing with golden highlights.

Brown hair was the standard in my family. Most of us had brown eyes, too, except for my grandma on my father's side. Her eyes are this rare shade of grey just like mine.

"I've got a job interview and I need to leave in a few minutes. Please, Achille, you won't forget, will you?" she asked, worried.

Mom knew I didn't like to take my sister to school because it meant I would have to walk, given that Aurora wasn't allowed to ride on my bike with me.

But that's only because one time we fell off and Aurora hit her chin. She still had a small scar to remind her of the accident.

"I'll remember," I promised.

A job interview. Mom had been trying to get back to work ever since she had been fired from the law firm where she had worked for twelve years, but she hadn't been able to find a job. The economy is terrible, she would say. I think that must be the tenth interview she had gone to in the past year, but so far she hadn't had any luck. In

the meantime, mom was working as a cleaning lady in some homes of Pieve Olimpia.

"What about dad?" I asked.

"He left very early this morning. Remo's mare is about to have her foal."

My dad Cesare is a vet. Remo Dionigi owns a huge farm with horses, cows and pigs, making him one of dad's biggest customers.

Mom planted a kiss first on my sister's forehead then on mine, and practically ran out.

I finished breakfast and took Aurora's and my bowl to the sink.

"Get dressed because we have to leave soon. And brush your teeth," I told her. Aurora pretended not to hear, so I turned off the TV.

"Humph," she huffed before poking her tongue out and running off to her room, yelling like crazy.

At ten to eight I told Aurora I was ready and she should get a move on.

I went out in the yard to wait for her. It was a beautiful sunny day and the spring air was pleasantly cool.

The first to notice me was a black and white cat named Oscar, who hurried over and started rubbing against my legs. A moment later a pretty ginger cat named Rusty came running up with her two kittens, Pippo and Nemo. The last to arrive was Pluto, a two-year-old mutt of some unidentifiable mixed breed. He was kind of ugly, but smart and I liked him. However, he avoided coming too close because he didn't find the sight of the cats very reassuring.

I love animals. I love all animals and they love me back; I know they do because I can read their thoughts, almost as if they were talking to me.

You're probably smirking and maybe someone is laughing at me. But believe me, I'm not crazy. I've never really told anyone because one time I tried telling my best friend, Giulio Nicoli, and he made that face at me... I could see from the way he grinned that he didn't believe me and thought I was teasing him. A bit like the face I imagine you're making right now. But it's the truth.

Believe it or not.

I don't remember the exact moment when I realized I could do it.

One thing is certain, I can't forget that time mom took me to the circus. I was five. I cried the whole time I was there, so we left the big top half way through the show. My mom asked what was wrong; I told her I could feel that the animals were suffering. She tried in vain to reassure me that the animals were actually treated well and cared for, but I knew it wasn't true. At least I knew they weren't happy. Elephants, chimpanzees and lions, as well as giraffes, tigers and zebras; being aware of their thoughts, I had grasped that the animals were sad and uncomfortable. Even my mom, who loves me very much, didn't seem to believe what I was saying and attributed it to a child's imagination.

But it was true!

About a year later it happened again when I went to fetch a ball that Giulio had kicked over a fence into the Filippis' yard. I wouldn't have climbed over the fence if anyone had been home, but I knew they weren't there. However, what I didn't remember was that they had a pit bull named Maciste, that they let roam freely in the yard when the family was out of town for a few days. I had heard Maciste was a bad dog because he had frightened and chased off many postmen, door-to-door salesmen and other bothersome people. By the time Giulio tried to remind me, it was too late. I had taken only a few steps when I found myself face-to-face with Maciste. He was growling at me, and baring his fearsome teeth.

I thought I was a goner; however, in that moment I could feel all Maciste needed was to be petted. His owner hardly ever petted him. I sat cross-legged on the lawn and spread my arms as if I wanted to hug him. Maciste came towards me, sniffed me and then he let me pet him like a puppy. Giulio couldn't believe his eyes. Although Giulio saw everything, when I tried to explain how I was able to do it, he didn't believe me for a moment.

Since then, I've never spoken about my ability again.

My sister's school is in downtown Pieve Olimpia, between the town hall and the post office; it's a fifteen-minute walk from our house. I took Aurora to the entrance before heading rapidly to my own school. On the way, I stopped by Mrs. Grimoldi's bakery to buy a focaccia for my mid-morning snack. A focaccia is an Italian flatbread, like a pizza crust, and you can put different things on it, but I like mine plain.

I waved to Mr. Nenni, who was already at his guard post on the bench in front of the gardens, ready for another long day of watching what little traffic went through the town. I dashed up the sidewalk, overtaking Mrs. Paoletti without saying anything because the lady had lost her hearing, not to mention quite a bit of her memory. I smiled at her, but she didn't respond. Mrs. Paoletti must have left her dentures at home. I hurried, almost running, and got to school just as the bell started ringing.

"Hi Aki," Giulio greeted me as I sat at my desk beside him. "You're late."

"Hi. I had to take Aurora to school," I justified myself.

"Ugh, sisters." He looked disgusted like he'd eaten a huge spoon of banana yogurt. He really hates banana yogurt. Giulio always complained that his two sisters, one older and one younger, wouldn't leave him alone and he often quarreled with them.

Friday lessons started with Mr. Doldi's math class. Ermanno Doldi was middle-aged, with wisps of unruly hair and an unkempt beard; he wore a green corduroy jacket that often smelled of fried food. I didn't like math; things like minimum common denominators and maximum common divisors made my head hurt. But Mr. Doldi was a good teacher who wasn't too strict when handing out grades.

"My dear Achille Chiorri," he said, "it's your turn to be quizzed today."

I had only a few days left in the school year to make up for a lackluster performance.

Probably in an attempt to help us relax, Mr. Doldi called us "dear" when he quizzed us; however, it didn't work very well with me because oral quizzes always made me feel sick to my stomach. I didn't do too badly, but not great either, so I ended up getting a score of six and a half out of ten, bringing my average for the year just barely up to six. But that's all I needed to avoid summer school in the company of fractions and powers.

Nobody beat me in English, though. I could speak it as fluently as a native. I was a natural. However, I preferred science and geography with Ms. Sandra Mazzei, one of the younger teachers. But even more than that, I liked the history class with Ms. Elide Bonelli, the oldest teacher in my school. Although she was almost sixty, she dressed youthfully and always wore a scarf around her neck. She had lots of scarves in many different colors. I liked how Ms. Bonelli taught history, but I was one of only a few students who were interested in the subject. Some of my classmates really disliked Ms. Bonelli, even to the point of ridiculing her for her excessively teased blond hair and the lipstick that often stained her front teeth.

At the break, we went out to the front yard. We were allowed to go there in the spring and summer, but only if it wasn't raining because the janitors complained when we returned carrying mud and dirt on our shoes. As was the case at least three days a week, Giulio had forgotten his snack at home, so I offered him a piece of my focaccia before joining a small group of laughing classmates. There were also two older boys from 2B who were angry with Paolo Morsini, nicknamed Greasy because his sweatshirt was always full of stains. They had taken his snack and were tossing it to each other as if it were a basketball. Greasy was an easy target. He was a skinny kid who always cried when something upset him. I didn't like that sort of game and I didn't think it was funny at all. But there was nothing I could do about it, so I walked away, dragging along Giulio who seemed glued to the spot and just stared at them. One day I had tried to interfere, but for days afterwards during the break those two guys from 2B made a habit of picking on me. I remember how I hated them.

Lilith was sitting on the only bench in the yard. She was from 1B, a class in the other division. As usual, she was sitting on her own, looking frail and nervous, while eating an orange. I walked over and sat down next to her. Hardly anyone at school would do that, so naturally it made me the brunt of many jokes; even Giulio teased me about it.

Lilith came from Syria and didn't speak Italian very well yet because she had arrived only a few months earlier, in the middle of the school year; but we understood each other perfectly. And I loved hanging out with her. With any other girl it would have been totally different, but I didn't want anything to do with any of them. Generally, I didn't like girls very much.

When our knees touched I didn't feel awkward and neither did Lilith because she didn't attempt to move away. She wasn't my girlfriend; not that I would have minded, but I didn't dare ask her. If she refused I would no longer be able to sit next to her.

We chatted while she finished eating her orange, then the bell rang and we had to go back to class. It was Friday so I told her to meet me back at the bench on Monday. I doubted that I would see her over the weekend because Lilith seldom went out and she was always with her parents.

On Fridays, Ms. Bonelli's class was the last one of the day. She sat at her desk, adjusted her light green scarf and made sure we were all there before beginning the lesson. The teacher informed us that we were ahead of our class schedule, so during this period she had decided to talk to us about something that wasn't in our textbook, but would be useful in helping us understand the history of the Middle Ages. The sound of hushed groans rose up from the class and someone mimicked throwing up. I was one of the few who listened attentively. "I will talk about the Vikings," began Ms. Bonelli. From the back of the room Michele Frati exclaimed "whatever" so loudly that I wonder the teacher didn't hear him.

"The Viking Age is traditionally the period characterized by the expansion of Northern Germanic populations, beginning from the first documented lootings of 790 through to the Norman Conquest of England in 1066. The Vikings themselves were Normans, except that Vikings proper were those Normans stationed along the Scandinavian coasts protected from the fjords; the Vikings' main activity was piracy...," I found the history of the Viking era fascinating.

After the last lesson of the day ended as usual at 2:00 pm, I went home for lunch. Many shops and businesses, like my dad's clinic,

are closed at lunchtime. When I got home, from the expression on my mother's face I could tell she wasn't holding out much hope regarding the outcome of her job interview. She dismissed my questions, saying that she wasn't really interested in the job anyway and so she wouldn't have minded if they didn't ask her to go back. However, I think she was a little upset. I told mom about my math grade, but not even that seemed to make her much happier.

Dad was also home, eating lunch with his head bent over his plate. I realized they had quarreled about work again.

I knew exactly what had happened because I'd seen it before: my dad would tell my mom not to worry and not to get upset because we were doing just fine. Mom would get annoyed and respond that she didn't want to stay home, that it was something she wanted to do for herself just to keep busy. My father would say that the family was already a demanding job and mom would argue that she needed to do more than that. "You just don't understand," she would finally snap; then, they would both sulk for a day and a half.

I quickly finished my lunch and went out with dad who had promised Remo that he would go back in the afternoon to check on the two newborn foals. I was happy to go with dad, except we almost ended up having to bring Aurora.

I got into the car; it was an old station wagon that had over eighty thousand miles on it and smelled of dog fur. Dad couldn't bring himself to get rid of it because he said the old car still did an honorable service.

"What do I need a new car for? This one's more than sufficient for my needs. When we want to go on a road trip we can take your mother's," he would say, knowing very well that we hardly ever went anywhere.

That was typical of my dad, who was a hard worker and didn't care for anything fancy. Same thing goes for his appearance. Although dad had just turned forty, he looked a bit older, mainly thanks to his old-fashioned glasses and the white hair that grew plentifully at his temples. He often wore pants and jackets in different shades of gray, and sometimes would match them with dull-colored ties. Mom once bought him a yellow tie, but a few months later it had

disappeared from dad's closet. What happened to it is still a mystery.

To reach Remo's property, we had to drive through Pieve Olimpia from one end to the other and it sure wasn't a long trip. We live in a small town that you can easily ride all round on your bike, yet we have everything we need: the town hall, a library, schools, a post office, a doctor's office and dad's veterinary clinic; we also had notaries and lawyers, a gas station, a game room and a supermarket, as well as shops and convenience stores. Oh yes, there's also a movie theater but it hardly ever shows first run movies.

A few years ago my parents had considered leaving Pieve Olimpia to move to a bigger city but in the end they decided against it. The fact that both my parents were born here probably weighed on their decision to stay.

And I'm glad they did.

We had reached Remo's. The foals were both well, just a little scared.

That's what I read in their thoughts.

TWO
HEIR TO THE SUPERIOR BEINGS

On Saturday mornings, free from school, I would often go to the clinic with dad while mom took Aurora with her to the grocery store or to the shops downtown.

However, on that particular Saturday for some reason Aurora was acting out. She didn't want to get up or have breakfast, then she didn't want to get dressed, then she starting yelling, then crying... You get the picture... What a pain! Finally, she insisted on staying with dad so we had to change our usual Saturday morning routine.

I was forced to go with mom to the grocery store. There was no use trying to protest. Given the atmosphere at home, I would have been taking a big risk.

My mother's sedan was clean and smelled fresh, nothing like the inside of dad's car that made me smell like I had spent a whole day in a dog kennel. "Darn, I almost forgot," she exclaimed, as we were about to reach the supermarket.

"What?" I asked.

She looked at the dashboard clock. "I had promised to go to Mr. Filippotti's this morning," she replied.

Mom quickly turned off the road we were on and drove back in the opposite direction.

Mr. Filippotti's home was just outside of Pieve Olimpia, a bit isolated from the town. In fact, he lived on the edge of the vast wooded area that surrounded our town and stretched as far as the eye could see to the valleys and the neighboring mountains.

I was quite happy with this unexpected change of plans.

I knew Archimede Filippotti because I had already been to his house before. He was a very old man but I didn't know his exact age. Undoubtedly, he was really, really old. He had snow-white hair, with a long matching white beard and a pair of intense brown eyes that seemed to be thousands of years old, like those of a person who had seen it all and knew everything. Usually, he would wear a tunic. It fell short of his bare feet and ankles that stuck out pale as the moon and full of tiny veins. With a longer beard and a pointy hat, he would have looked just like Merlin the Magician in the Disney cartoon, one of Aurora's favorite characters. His voice was warm like a summer day and sometimes it sounded almost hypnotic. He owned a fantastic collection of antiques. There were Egyptian, Greek and Roman artifacts that he guarded jealously and he only let a few people see them. But only to look at, not to touch. I was one of the lucky few allowed to see them.

I was almost forgetting about his love for cats. He had dozens of them; small and large, black, ginger, white, spotted, tabby, longhaired and shorthaired. Not even Mr. Filippotti himself knew the exact number of cats that roamed everywhere, in and around the house. He would even call them all by name, but I think he was bluffing a bit.

It would have been impossible to remember them all!

Despite the many cats that ran around everywhere, his house was pretty clean, thanks to my mother who did the housework a couple of times a week.

We arrived at the house - a cottage in urgent need of maintenance. The plaster was peeling off in several places and the gutter hung so precariously that I feared it might fall off at any moment.

Mom parked and we were greeted by a swarming tide of cats that rubbed against our legs and jumped on the car. They ran in front of us up to the house, as if they wanted to announce that we had arrived. Mr. Filippotti opened the door and greeted us with a smile.

"Good morning, Virginia. Ah, I see you've brought your dear son. What a pleasure, Achille... You have an important name, Achilles, like the great mythological hero and warrior from ancient Greece. What do your friends call you... Aki, isn't it?" he asked, ruffling my hair with his bony hand.

"Yes, Mr. Filippotti," I replied shyly. He always welcomed me in the same way.

"Come, come in," he said and motioned us to enter as a dozen cats came running out while just as many went running in. "What terrible cats," he exclaimed with a burst of laughter.

Although the house was quite clean and didn't smell, for my mom it was a nightmare because it was a total mess everywhere. A pile of dishes rose up from the sink like the tower of Pisa and only a miracle of the laws of physics prevented it from collapsing. Cans and packs of cat food were stacked on the sparse furniture and on the floor. Cat fur was everywhere. Fur bunnies rolled around the floor while entire coils of cat fur were stuck to the many rugs scattered throughout the house. Books and magazines were stacked all over the place: in the living room and the bedroom, in the hallway and in the study. The study... That was the only room mom did not have to clean and tidy up. And thank goodness!

The room wasn't very big, but it seemed even smaller because it was unbelievably packed with so much stuff. Books were everywhere, even more so than in the other rooms. The bookcase looked like it might burst at any moment, with piles of books so high as to almost reach the ceiling. The desk was buried under a deep layer of pages covered with Mr. Filippotti's incomprehensible handwriting. Some of the pages even covered the keyboard of an old computer that I had never seen turned on. It probably didn't even work anymore, used only by the cats sleeping peacefully on the monitor. The window shutters always remained closed and the room's only illumination came from the dim light of a lamp. Behind the desk was a locked door leading down to a large basement where Mr. Filippotti kept his collection of precious antiquities.

"Come with me Aki. Let your mother work her magic and bring order to this chaos," he said, inviting me to follow him into the study. I enjoyed being with the old man because he knew a lot of amazing stories that made me lose track of time. As I listened to his tales, I felt like I was traveling to distant places and other times in history.

He sat at his desk while I sat down on the rug in front of him. A longhaired gray cat settled in my lap. His name was Timoteo, and he was one of my favorites. Timoteo was suspicious of humans and aggressive towards his peers, but he was affectionate with me. He purred while letting me pet him. I knew that he liked to hang out with me - I had read his thoughts.

He was thinking the same thing this day, too.

"I like cuddling with you, too," I told him and his purring became more intense.

Mr. Filippotti smiled.

"Do you like my stories?" he asked.

"Very much," I exclaimed. "I'd love to hear every one of them."

"Who knows, maybe one day we'll get there, but first you have to become as old as I am."

"Then I guess I'll have to wait a bit. How old are you, anyway?" I

asked just to get an idea of how long I would have to wait.

He didn't answer me. Actually, he seemed to be considering it; that's funny, I thought to myself. It was an easy question. Who doesn't remember how old they are?

"Oh, I wasn't talking about age, but about wisdom and knowledge; that takes a long, long time," he told me.

I didn't understand and I thought he was just trying to avoid the question. Yet, it seemed a pretty innocent question!

"Have I ever shown you the Sphere of Time?" he asked, shrewdly changing the topic.

"No," I said, not having a clue what it was.

"Come, let's go," he cried as he stood up. I followed him. "You can come too, Timoteo," he added and the cat followed us.

He turned the latch and we went down to the basement. Mr. Filippotti walked along and tackled the stairs with the agility of a much younger man.

Right, but how old was he?

It was a mystery.

He flipped a switch and several spotlights instantly came on, lighting up the spacious room. Although it was almost summer, down there it was totally freezing. The artifacts, divided by age and civilization, were preserved in glass cases. It was such an amazing collection that I had often wondered if he hadn't stolen the items from a museum. There were amphorae and statues from the ancient Greek civilization, Roman helmets, weapons and armor, reproductions of deities dating back to the Ancient Egyptian era, artifacts from Mesopotamia and many more. Compared to the last time he had brought me down to his private museum, the artifacts seemed to have grown in number.

I couldn't believe it!

I followed him without saying a word, getting huge goose bumps as we walked among the display cases. I was freezing to death. Timoteo ran past us and stopped at the foot of a pedestal about three feet tall, where he waited as if he knew where we were headed. In fact, that's exactly where we stopped, too.

On top of the pedestal was a globe-shaped object the size of a

19

soccer ball, black as coal and so bright you couldn't look at it for more than a few seconds.

"That's it. The Sphere of Time," announced Mr. Filippotti.

"Interesting," I said, turning away to avoid blinding myself.
"So where does it come from?"
"From many places," he replied.
"What do you mean...," I started to ask, but he interrupted me.
"Lay your hands on it."

I hesitated. Mr. Filippotti was very protective of his collection. This was the first time he had ever given me permission to touch anything. I had so wanted to touch the Roman military weapons or the Spartan helmet, but he was adamant: no, no and no.

I put one hand on the Sphere.

"Both hands."

I obeyed.

The surface felt warm as if it had just been washed with hot water and it was perfectly smooth like glass.

Mr. Filippotti gave me a curious look and frowned.

"Don't you feel anything?" he asked somewhat annoyed.

"A little heat... Nothing special," I replied.

Just as I finished saying those words, the Sphere changed color, turning bright orange as if a fire were burning on the inside. I felt its temperature rising, but I couldn't pull my hands away – they might as well have been glued to the Sphere. Suddenly I became dizzy and everything starting spinning. I closed my eyes so I wouldn't vomit. I wanted to cry out but I couldn't because I was shaking like a leaf and my mouth wouldn't open.

Help!

Then suddenly a whole stack of images began to pass before my eyes. I saw the Roman legions fighting against bearded barbarians, men and animals carrying huge blocks of stone to be used in the construction of a pyramid, scenes of life around a temple in ancient Greece, religious ceremonies on the top of a Babylonian temple, and so many more scenes, all in a whirlwind of noise and colors, and sounds and smells. It all seemed so credible, so real.

As suddenly as it had begun, in an instant it was over. I opened my eyes.

My hands were no longer resting on the Sphere as Mr. Filippotti, clasping my wrists, had pulled them up.

"Wow! How cool!" I exclaimed, try to catch my breath.

"Then you saw..."

"I saw? Heck, there are a lot of crazy things in there. Better than any video game. But how is it possible?"

He smiled. His eyes were sparkling with triumph. "I wasn't

wrong. You are one of the Heirs. Timoteo had noticed, too," he added.

I looked at him as if he had burped during Christmas mass. "Heirs? Timoteo? What are you talking about?"

"Very few people, only the Heirs, in fact, can see what you have seen."

"Heirs? Heirs to whom... To what?" I wanted to know. His words were confusing me.

"The Heirs to the powers and knowledge of the Ancients."

"And I... I'm supposed to be a... I'm supposed to be an heir to the power of the Ancients? But what does it mean? I don't understand any of it!"

"Yes, you are."

"Knowledge... What knowledge? Heck, I can barely get a passing grade at school. If not for Mr. Doldi, I would have flunked math."

"Do you know anyone else who can read the minds of animals?"

"No... Actually, I don't think I do."

"You see, then?"

"So that would be my superpower?"

"You certainly have others that you will discover with time - and don't call them superpowers."

"Which ones will I have?"

"I don't know. I don't know what the Ancients have in store for you."

"Still with these Ancients. But who are you talking about?"

"The Superior Beings."

"I still don't get it."

"They are the Beings that govern the energy of Nature and of humans."

"You're giving me a headache. I don't understand any of it! Believe me, I don't have any powers. I'm a totally normal kid."

"What about the Sphere of Time, then? Only you and the other Heirs can see what you saw."

"Who are the others?"

"I don't know."

"You mean that if any of my friends put their hands on it nothing will happen unless they are one of the Heirs?"

He nodded. "That's right."

"But if I tell people something like that they'll think I'm a wacko," I protested.

"You must never tell anyone about what happened to you or the things you saw."

"What? I don't think so! I have to tell Giulio. He'll be so envious."

"You will not do it," he ordered, raising his voice. "It must remain a secret."

"Okay, okay, don't get angry, I won't tell anyone. But it's a shame. Can't I even tell my sister?"

"Nobody."

"My mom?"

"N-O, no!" he repeated.

"Okay, so why did you let me do it? It's no fun if I can't tell anyone."

"It will be useful to you, for your own knowledge."

"My what? Oh, is this what you meant when you spoke of wisdom and knowledge?"

"Yes, but not only that."

"So does that mean I can repeat the experience and see all those images again?"

"Yes, but I must warn you about something."

"What?"

"Next time it will last much longer and you will be transported to another dimension," he said gravely.

He looked worried, but I thought it was crazy cool.

"The Sphere of Time is a very powerful artifact; however, I don't have complete control of its power. Not yet, at least, which means I'm not able to tell you where you'll be transported or what will happen to you. I must warn you, it could be very dangerous."

I took his warning with a grain of salt. What could be so dangerous? It was like going to the movies, only that the images appeared more real. You could almost touch the things that revolved around you. A bit better than 3D movies.

"I'm ready. I'll be careful," I replied without really knowing what

could be so dangerous.

I put my hands on the Sphere.

Timoteo hopped onto my shoulders.

"Hey...," I exclaimed.

"Don't ever get separated from him."

Then everything started spinning around me.

THREE
TROLL!!!

Cold.

Cold.

So cold.

"Mr. Filippotti, it's too cold down here. You should think about heating it up a bit," I told him.

Although I imagined that my hands were still on the Sphere of Time, I managed to open my eyes.

Surprise...

Awesome surprise!

I wasn't at Mr. Filippotti's. I was sitting in a meadow and my jeans were getting wet on the damp grass. I saw a forest of tall trees to my right and snowy mountains straight ahead. I wasn't familiar with this place - it certainly wasn't anywhere near Pieve Olimpia. I didn't recognize anything.

Timoteo was there, too. He stood by my side and showed no signs of fear.

That's weird for a cat.

"Where are we?" I asked him.

He replied with a meow, and I realized he didn't know either.

I got up.

"Mr. Filippotti," I shouted and heard the echo of my voice spread far and away.

"Now I get it. It's all very real. You can wake me up now."

No one answered.

"Mr. Filippotti, I have to do my homework," I called out hoping that this would convince him to act.

I gathered up Timoteo and closed my eyes. I was sure that when I opened them again I would be back in my strange friend's basement.

I opened one.

Nothing had changed. I shut it again and counted to a hundred.

"In a minute I'll open my eyes," I said, hoping that Mr. Filippotti could hear me.

I opened the other eye and then closed it again.

It wasn't working.

And it was beginning to rain, too.

I opened my eyes, but the landscape around me had not changed. Now what?

It was no use remaining glued to the spot in the steadily increasing rain, so I set out in search of shelter. I started walking cautiously down a trail, with Timoteo following me.

"I must never be separated from you...," I said.

"Why not? Answer me... Come on, think something... Tell me why you should be so important," I snapped.

"You're telling me there will be plenty of time... For what? Well, go on, tell me what's happening," I snarled at him, but Timoteo kept walking, ignoring my questions. All at once he began running, forcing me to do the same as I struggled to keep up.

Then suddenly he came to a dead halt, flattened his ears and hissed at something in the vegetation alongside the trail. Panting, I caught up with him and then...

A strong, dull gray colored arm lifted me off the ground and dangled me in mid-air. I tried to see who the arm belonged to and...

Help! How scary!

It was... It was... It was a troll!

It stood over six feet tall, bald-headed with two beady, menacing eyes. He was wearing only a pair of green breeches and studded leather cuffs. He smelled weird, like a mix of moss and wet ashes from the fireplace.

"Fiú flý j," he croaked.

I was too shocked to notice that he had just told me to flee in Old Norse and that I had actually understood what he said.

In fact, I replied: "Minn köttr."

Obviously, that huge, gray thing understood me because he reached out with his other arm to grab Timoteo, who began hissing and growling. He tried to sink his claws into the troll's hand but couldn't make a scratch, as if it were nothing more than the sting of an insect.

I could understand Norse. Was this one of the powers that Mr.

26

Filippotti had talked about? I didn't even have time to wonder why I would need to understand the language of the Vikings, when the troll put me down and handed me Timoteo.

Then the troll crouched down in the tall grass and motioned me with his huge finger to be quiet.

Although my legs were shaking, I didn't try to escape. In fact, I squatted down beside him as I struggled to hold on to Timoteo.

The troll gave Timoteo such a grim look that I was afraid he wanted to throw a punch at the cat. I figured the troll must have been monstrously strong and one of his blows would have turned Timoteo into a furry meatball.

"Why are we hiding?" I asked. It seemed impossible that such a creature would be afraid of anything. Being so big and looking so fierce, what could he be afraid of?

"Great threat," he replied.

"Threat? What threat?" I wanted to know. By now I was speaking Norse fluently, without even realizing it.

Too bad Norse wasn't part of the school curriculum.

"Muspellsmegir," he replied.

Fire Giants.

For a moment I thought he was kidding. How could there be creatures larger than him?

But then I felt the earth tremble slightly, like the tremor caused by an earthquake. Only there was more than one tremor. The first was followed by another, and then another until the cause became obvious. The tremors were being made by the footsteps of the gigantic creature I could see coming down the trail.

I don't know how tall he was, but probably about as high as a four-story building and he was... He was all up in flames. That's right, it was like he was made of fire.

I was so scared I almost wet my pants, while Timoteo jumped from my arms and fled off to hide in the woods. I was hoping I'd be able to find him otherwise Mr. Filippotti would never let me hear the end of it.

Boom, boom, boom...

Each step vibrated along the ground.

He kept coming closer until he passed right by us. So close I could feel the heat radiating from his body. It was burning with a red-hot fire.

His footsteps vibrated all the way up into my head and made my teeth chatter. The troll's eyes were wide with fear as he clapped his hands over ears as big as an elephant's.

The giant creature moved beyond us and I breathed a sigh of relief. Just as the troll raised his head to make sure that the giant was moving away, we heard a noise coming from the forest. A broken branch, a fallen boulder... I didn't know what to make of the noise, but the giant heard it and stopped. He turned back in our direction and his eyes, red as the sun at dawn, glowed as they focused on us.

"Fireballs," shouted the troll and started running.

Before I had time to wonder what he meant, I saw the giant throw a flaming ball the size of a truck wheel.

I raced off just as the fireball seemed to explode at my back. The troll moved quickly with the gait of a huge chimpanzee, running nimbly through the trees and bushes. I stumbled through the undergrowth, struggling to keep up with him.

I heard an explosion behind me and I sensed that it must have been another fireball launched by the giant. We ran deeper into the dense forest where the giant couldn't follow us, until I was out of breath and had to stop. My arms dangling at my sides, I bent over exhausted.

I looked back. The giant hadn't followed us, but I could see in the distance a few columns of smoke where the fireballs had fallen.

We had made it.

The troll didn't notice I had stopped and kept running until I lost sight of him. But at least Timoteo was there, appearing at my side after popping out from a clump of shrubs.

"Where did you come from?" I asked.

Meow.

"You're right, you were smarter than us because you hid before the fire monster got there."

I caught my breath, wondering what else to expect after the troll and the fire giant.

"I want to go back," I cried, knowing it probably wouldn't happen.

The Sphere of Time had catapulted me into an unknown world and now I didn't know how to get back home. I was hoping that at least Mr. Filippotti knew what to do, although I clearly remembered him saying that he still hadn't learned how to control the Sphere's powers.

So did that mean I would have to stay in this strange place forever? The thought gave me goose bumps and it made me want to cry. I looked around.

Which way should I go?

There was no way I could go back down the trail. Too dangerous. So, let's go straight ahead. Or what about right, or left? Beats me. All the forest looked the same.

Timoteo solved the problem; he decided to leave and headed off to the left.

"Hey, wait," I protested and followed him, hoping that he wouldn't lead me into further trouble.

Although it had stopped raining, by now I was already soaked from head to toe. My sweatshirt and jeans were totally drenched and my feet were sloshing in my sneakers. My teeth were chattering from the cold.

I followed Timoteo to goodness knows where through the woods, until I heard lapping in the distance. Was it a river or stream?

After a short while, Timoteo stopped. When I reached him, I saw that we were practically out of the forest and standing at the edge of a rocky cliff with a sheer face that fell into a vast expanse of water. I couldn't make out the water's boundaries so I figured it was a kind of sea. But I had no clue which sea it could have been.

"Great, Timoteo, excellent choice. From here we have absolutely nowhere to go. We have to go back. Come on, let's get moving."

The words had hardly left my mouth when Timoteo sped off like a rocket, fleeing again into the woods.

"Timoteo," I called, but it was no use because I had lost sight of him. I didn't even try to chase after him.

Now what?

I was back to square one. I didn't know where to go, what to look for and, the most important thing of all, how to get back to Pieve Olimpia.

I checked my watch. It had stopped.

As I sat down on the grass looking out to sea, a ray of sunshine

peeked out through the clouds, bringing me a little warmth.

My situation was desperate to say the least and I didn't even know who to ask for help. Apart from monstrous creatures, there didn't seem to be anyone else around here.

Famous last words.

"Don't move," someone ordered me in Old Norse. It sounded like the voice of a boy.

I remained seated.

I heard the sound of many footsteps behind me. Whoever had spoken wasn't alone.

"Can I turn around?" I asked, as I turned without waiting for an answer.

There were five of them. Four boys and a girl. All blond with light colored eyes, mostly green, but some were blue. The boys must have been about my age while the girl was probably not much older than Aurora. The boys were wearing a tunic over their trousers and the girl was wearing a dress that came down almost to her ankles. They were all barefoot.

I stood up and the oldest of the group pointed a sharp, spear-like wooden stick at me.

"Keep away," he ordered.

They looked at me as if I was a mysterious creature and that's probably just how I appeared to them, especially because of my clothes and my shoes.

"Who are you?" the leader of the group asked me.

"My name is Achille Chiorri."

When they heard my name they looked at each other. Someone tried to pronounce it but it came out as a bunch of incomprehensible, ridiculous sounds.

"You can call me Aki," I said, coming to their rescue.

This was easier to pronounce.

"Aki," each one repeated.

"Where are you from?" It was always the oldest who spoke.

Good question. What could I say?

I tried telling them the truth.

"I come from Pieve Olimpia."

Questioning faces looked back at me. This time, no one tried to repeat the name. Too complicated.

"I am a traveler and I come from that direction," I said, pointing at the forest behind them." I got lost in the woods after leaving the trail," I added.

I could see they didn't trust me. They kept their distance until the girl stopped hesitating and walked up to me.

"My name is Helga," she introduced herself.

Taken by surprise by the girl's action and miffed at being shown up by the courage of the youngest among them, the boys also came forward.

"Halldor," the oldest of the group introduced himself. He was also the tallest.

The others were Arni, who had protruding ears; Karli, who had a Mohawk haircut like many professional soccer players; and Broddi, with a face full of freckles as if someone had sprayed him with orange juice.

"Will you come with us?" asked Helga, who kept touching my jeans, fascinated by the fabric. On the other hand, Arni was attracted to my shoes and asked if he could try them on.

I told him he could. It was so funny to watch him walk then stumble and fall flat on his face.

"We are returning to the village; if you want, you can come with us," said Halldor.

I accepted.

After all, where else could I have gone?

At least they were human beings!

FOUR
A Viking Village in the Year 1000

I followed my new friends to a village situated at the head of a long fjord that penetrated inland. Sheltered from the icy winds, there were numerous wooden houses, some with a sloping roof while others were covered with grass turf. The village stood on a stretch of high ground that fell away to a pebbly beach and rocks overlooking the unfamiliar sea. A long pier had been built to allow the mooring and anchoring of ships.

I couldn't tell how many people were in the village, maybe a few dozen. They were all busy doing various activities. Some people were taking care of the cattle, others were fishing, selling products at their stalls, or busy with housework. There was also a group doing combat exercises.

I would learn that there was always a flurry of activity during the summer. But during the winter months full of frost and snow, the men preferred to remain under the covers and do nothing, leaving the women to deal with the housework.

When we reached the village, our small group broke up and I was left with Karli. As we walked along, the people stared at me. Some were just curious while others seemed to scrutinize me from head to toe. Although I'm not usually shy, the way they stared at me was embarrassing, as if they expected me to start twirling or perform like an acrobat from the circus.

"This is my home," Karli announced, pointing to a wooden building with a wisp of smoke coming out through the roof. I was stunned to see Timoteo up there. He was perched just above the door as if waiting for me. How had he managed to get there?

He sure was a special cat. In fact, I began to believe that he really did have some unknown power.

I went inside.

The house consisted of two rooms separated by a partial wooden wall. The larger room, with its fireplace, was used for cooking and eating, while the bedding on the floor of the smaller room made it

clear what it was used for.

I met Karli's mother, Gerrid, a blonde woman with strong arms and a stern look, who welcomed me a little suspiciously. For a minute I was afraid she might grab me by the hair and drag me out of her house.

Karli tried to explain who I was, but she never lost her wary expression.

How could I blame her!

I didn't know myself how to explain my presence in the land of the Vikings. Just thinking about it made me woozy.

"Those weird clothes of yours are wet," Karli said. "Here, put these on," he added, handing me a tunic and a pair of breeches.

The clothes were made of crude wool that immediately made me itch. I scratched as if I had fleas and my skin soon turned red like I had rubbed it with sandpaper.

I was itching like crazy!

I left my sneakers out to dry as well, so I had to put on a pair of sandals that looked like those worn by monks.

I felt pretty ridiculous, but at least people stopped staring at me like I belonged in freak show. I was glad not to be the center of annoying glances.

Karli took me for a walk around the village. I noticed that the place was full of dogs of all sizes and colors. My new friend explained that the dogs were necessary to fend off the wolves that inhabited the woods.

We walked through the market where they sold all sorts of products, from roosters and hens, to tools and animal skins. As we passed by a tavern I saw men drinking an amber colored liquid while playing a game similar to chess. We came to a stop in front of a rather large building that, Karli informed me, was the residence of the jarl, the village chief.

He was unsuccessfully trying to explain to me who the current jarl's ancestors were, when we heard sounds of a commotion.

The shouts of "they're back, they're back" were passed rapidly from person to person until a whole crowd had gathered, hurrying to the pier.

"Our warriors are back. Let's hope they brought in a good haul," said Karli, as we joined the people heading towards the sea.

Moments later, two Viking ships had already docked.

The ships were loaded with all the war booty. And from what I could see, there was plenty of it. Not only were there gold and silver artifacts and precious stones, but also animal skins, weapons, fabrics and even food supplies. The western raids had proved so successful they were already making plans to go back as soon as possible. Having returned from a successful mission, the warriors raved about all the incredibly wealthy people and cities full of treasures, a paradise for looters and plunderers.

Listening to these stories took me back to Ms. Bonelli's lesson on the Vikings. She had explained how, in the early ninth century, the Vikings had carried out numerous raids along the English coast, conquering a vast section of England over the course of the following centuries. I wondered if that was in fact the time period into which the Sphere of Time had transported me. From what the warriors were saying, it seemed that the coasts where they had landed were still largely unknown. If my hunch was correct, it meant that the Sphere of Time was some sort of time machine.

So why did Mr. Filippotti talk about Heirs, Ancients, and Superior Beings? About powers and knowledge? About Nature's Energy and Human Energy?

It didn't make any sense.

It would have been much easier if he had told me up front:

"Dear Aki, I have discovered how to travel through the ages. Get ready to travel through time."

If you think I would have refused, you are totally mistaken. The idea of time travel had always fascinated me; in fact, I thought it would have been a blast!

I had often daydreamed that I was strolling around the pyramids, or fighting alongside a Roman legionary, or witnessing a duel between medieval knights. Just imagine, my dream had come true. Who wouldn't want that to happen?

However, I wasn't sure that things were quite that "simple"

because surely Mr. Filippotti hadn't just been talking nonsense. I suspected there was more that I had yet to find out. And it was a good thing that I realized it.

Because there was actually a lot more to be discovered.

The Viking warriors were just as I had imagined them.

Big men with bushy beards, most of them had long hair and a fierce look about them. They were armed with axes, clubs, swords and spears, wore leather armor and carried a colored shield strapped to one arm. But one thing surprised me and I bet it will surprise all of you: the Vikings' helmets didn't have horns. I'm absolutely certain about it because I didn't see even one helmet with horns.

Actually, the helmets were generally shaped like a cap reinforced with a metallic crest. Some had neck guards and others had cheek plates, but there was no trace of horns.

I decided that, if I ever managed to get back to Pieve Olimpia, I would ask Ms. Bonelli why we believed Viking helmets had horns. Maybe she would know.

Karli's father had also participated in the western mission. His name was Bjarni; from the way everyone showed respect, I figured he must have been a warrior chief. His chest and powerful arms were totally covered in scars; some were small, like cigarette burns, while some of the bigger ones had so much scar tissue it made me uncomfortable to look at them. Like his son, Bjarni wore his hair long at the back while the sides of his head were shaved. His thick beard was fashioned into a braid that started from his chin and fell the length of a span.

He greeted his wife and son with hugs and kisses and when Karli tried to introduce me, he turned away to exchange laughs and slaps on the back with another man as big as himself. After returning home from a long night of celebrations, Bjarni continued to totally ignore me. He must have been too drunk to notice the bundle lying next to the fireplace where he stumbled, almost falling over. Well, that bundle was me, trying to get some sleep under an old flea infested blanket. But even though I was exhausted, I couldn't fall asleep. I felt terribly alone, and I missed home. Timoteo quietly slipped under the blanket beside me and began purring. It was comforting to be able to hug him. I wondered if my mother was worried about my disappearance.

What had Mr. Filippotti told her, I asked myself. I missed her smile, I missed the loving things she always said to me before turning off the light and wishing me goodnight. I missed Aurora and dad, too. And Giulio. And Lilith, although I would never have admitted it. I knew they would all be worried about me and I had no way of letting them know that, despite everything, I was just fine. I gulped back the tears, I couldn't stay a minute longer in that house full of strangers. I stood up, grabbed my blanket and walked down to the beach with Timoteo at my side.

I sat down and wrapped us both up in the blanket. As I gazed at the light of the Moon and the stars reflecting off the placid waters of that unknown sea, I felt even sadder.

Suddenly, a dog appeared from the darkness and sat beside me. He must have sensed my sadness, because he rested his head on my shoulder.

The dog smelled like dad's car, making me feel sort of at home.

Then another dog arrived, then another one. Timoteo wasn't afraid of the dogs, and the dogs didn't seem to care about him, either. In the moonlight it was difficult to count them all, but there were quite of few them now. I understood from their thoughts that the dogs were there to comfort me and that made me feel better. Finally I was able to fall asleep.

I woke up to the sight of the dawn colors splashed across the sky. Timoteo was no longer there and neither were the dogs.

In their place stood a huge man towering over me.

"Yes, father, this is my traveler friend," Karli was saying. I could hear that he was nearby, but I didn't see him until I sat up. Arni, with his big ears, was there, too.

"Do those strange clothes belong to him?"

"Yes, they're his. His name is Aki."

I stretched and stood up, facing Bjarni. I'm one of the tallest kids in my class, but I only came up to his belly button. He grabbed me by the shoulders and lifted me as if I were a feather. He looked straight at me with his piercing green eyes. His braided beard tickled my nose, making me want to sneeze. Luckily, I was able to hold it in.

"Where are you from, Aki?" he asked.

I was dangling my legs like a puppet. It's a pretty uncomfortable position to be in when you're being interrogated.

"I came from the woods," I replied, while thinking he would be much harder to convince than Karli and the other kids.

"From the woods? And how did you get to the woods?"

"I got lost after leaving the trail," I answered.

My shoulders were beginning to hurt.

"Why did you happen to leave the trail right by our village?" he demanded.

He questioned me as though I were an enemy, a spy or just someone hostile to his people. I was getting scared. At this point, I decided to tell the truth even at the cost of seeming crazy. Who would believe in trolls and fire giants?

"It was a troll. I was walking along the path when a troll grabbed me and took me into the woods."

"A troll?"

No surprise that he didn't believe me.

"Yes," I insisted. "It was gray and had long arms."

Bjarni put me down.

"And where is the troll now?"

"He ran off into the forest when the fire giant came after us."

I was sure he was going to laugh, instead he gave me a hard look. His expression darkened.

"A fire giant?"

"That's right, we ran off when he started throwing exploding fireballs at us," I explained.

"I don't believe you."

"I figured you wouldn't. I know it sounds crazy, but that's exactly what happened."

I noticed Karli had turned very pale, while Arni seemed ready to burst into tears. I didn't understand their reaction. In their place, I would probably be rolling on the ground laughing.

"Would you be able to show me where he threw the fireballs?" asked Bjarni.

"Sure. As you go toward the path, it's easy to see scorched patches and burnt shrubs. That's where the fireballs fell. At first I was afraid they would set the whole forest on fire."

Bjarni didn't let me say anything else.

He ordered me to go home with his son and Arni to wait for his return. He wanted to make sure I had told the truth.

"Do not talk to anyone about this," he commanded sternly.

And I thought they were all going to make fun of me.

I obeyed and followed Karli, who was staring at me as though I had suddenly come down with some horrible disease. Not to mention Arni, who had started sniffling like a wuss.

Although Karli's mother realized that something had happened, she didn't ask any questions. She would wait for her husband to return and ask him about it.

Although Gerrid was still surly, she offered me something to eat. She filled a wooden bowl with something that tasted like soured milk and gave me a piece of dried meat that looked like a piece of wood. I wished that I had the usual milk and cereal I eat for breakfast. Since mom had lost her job, sometimes I got a slice of homemade cake, too.

I somehow managed not to throw up, and left everything on the table untouched. I hoped Karli's mother wouldn't think me rude, but that stuff was totally disgusting.

Luckily there was some fruit that I gobbled up as if it were the tastiest thing in the world.

Nobody said anything.

Gerrid went on with her housework. She kept throwing glances my way as if to make sure I hadn't magically vanished into thin air.

Karli and Arni seemed dumbfounded. They just stared at me but when I looked at them, they would quickly turn the other way.

Whatever!

I put my own clothes back on now that they were dry, and I felt much more comfortable.

I tried to say something, but no one paid attention.

"What's wrong with everyone?" I asked.

"Let's just wait for my father," said Karli.

"Why?"

"Because."

End of conversation.

I was getting bored, but as soon as I started towards the door Gerrid planted herself in front of me with a menacing stance, preventing me from going out. Ugh!

Finally we heard footsteps. Men came running towards the house. We heard the clamor of excited voices.

Bjarni entered the house. He looked really upset, as if he had just found out that his car had been stolen from his driveway.

"Ragnarok!" he exclaimed.

FIVE
THE TWO DWARVES

Ragnarok.

Ragnarok.

Ragnarok.

Suddenly, that word seemed to be on the lips of every person in the village; it was spoken with a mix of fear and awe.

Ragnarok.

Thanks to my unexpected knowledge of Norse, I was able to understand the meaning of the word that was something like, "Fate of the Gods."

It may not have been an exact translation but you get the idea, and it wasn't very reassuring. Judging by the way it upset everybody, I realized it must have been a pretty serious matter.

Karli explained that Ragnarok was the final battle of the gods, a sort of Armageddon, which explained all the unrest and concern.

I didn't know much about deities, but a battle among the gods seemed really serious, and when you added the word "final" it sounded very much like it would be the decisive reckoning.

Creepy stuff.

The Sphere of Time couldn't have chosen a worse time and place to transport me. Finding myself in the middle of a battle among gods was dangerous enough, but it wasn't my only problem. Before dealing with the fury of the gods, I had to face the anger of the villagers.

As soon as the news spread that I was the first person to have laid eyes on the fire giant, someone starting spreading the word that I brought bad luck. In the blink of an eye I found myself surrounded by people with very bad intentions.

I managed to sneak out and run away from a bunch of people who had it in for me, but I soon found the road blocked by bigger and angrier groups. Luckily, I was wearing my sneakers so I ran headlong toward the woods, hoping to get away.

But I soon realized that they wouldn't simply let me go.

I saw a screaming mob armed with axes and clubs running behind me.

Sure, I had finished second, behind a boy from 3A, in the two hundred meters track race at my school in Pieve Olimpia, but trying to get away from a herd of crazed Vikings who wanted my head was another matter altogether.

I had little hope of making it out of there.

Help!

Although I kept running as fast as I could, the distance between my fierce pursuers and myself kept getting smaller and smaller. I didn't turn around anymore, but I expected to find myself in an iron grip at any moment.

It was the end.

Goodbye mom and dad, goodbye Aurora, goodbye Giulio and all my friends, goodbye...

Suddenly, out of nowhere Timoteo came flying along beside me, fast as an arrow.

"Timoteo," I barely managed to get out, when suddenly the earth opened up beneath me. I fell into a hole and kept sliding down as if I had been riding in a water chute at the water park near my home.

Aaaaahhhhhhh!

I screamed like crazy as I continued to slide before slamming my butt on the hard ground and eating the dust I had raised around me.

Finally, I ended up on a bed of grass and leaves. Timoteo landed on my stomach. I waited a moment, but no one else came out of the tunnel.

Yuck! Yuck!

My mouth was full of dirt and I tried to spit some of it out.

"We're safe. That was really close," I cried, greatly relieved.

Timoteo agreed with me.

"How is it you always seem to appear out of nowhere?"

He didn't bother answering me and jumped off the bed of leaves.

I got up and leaped down beside him. I hurt all over, but it was nothing compared to what would have happened to me if I had ended up in the clutches of the Vikings. At the very least they would have ripped me into tiny pieces.

The grassy bed where I had landed was at least four feet high and twice as long. It seemed impossible that it just happened to be right where I needed it. Someone must have arranged for it to be there.

"Welcome," said someone behind me. I turned around but didn't see anyone.

"Look a little lower," said another voice.

I turned around and...

Two dwarves!

Obviously they were brothers because the resemblance was remarkable. They were a little over three feet tall... Short... They had bright, curious eyes and a little goatee beard. The only difference between the two dwarves was that one had an almost normal nose, while the other one had a nose that looked as if a big, lumpy potato had been placed in the middle of his face.

They wore Viking style trousers and tunics and each had a leather helmet pulled down over his head.

"We are Brokk..."

"... And Eitri."

"Pleased to meet you. I'm Aki. Thank you so much for saving me," I said.

"We couldn't let them hurt you," said Brokk, the one with the bigger nose.

"But how did you know...," I started to ask, but they didn't let me finish the sentence.

"Come, follow us. And bring your cat with you, of course," added Eitri.

But in the meantime, Timoteo had disappeared again.

I followed the two dwarves along a path that led into the forest, until we came to a gurgling stream.

We had arrived at our destination.

They lived in a house built into the rock and when I followed them in, I had to stoop to get through the door. Inside the house my head almost touched the stone ceiling, making me feel like a giant.

I sort of felt like Gulliver. However, the size of everything else, from the beds to the table, was normal and the house itself was spacious.

Brokk and Eitri were two blacksmiths and their shop was also built into the rock. I would have expected it to be rather small, but I was wrong; in fact, it was as wide as the gym at my school. A bed of glowing embers was burning in the furnace, which took up half the wall. Brokk operated the bellows, instantly rekindling the fire that spread a lot of heat everywhere.

Later the dwarves asked me if I was hungry. At first, I answered that I was, but immediately regretted it.

I couldn't forget that disgusting food Karli's mother had offered me. I asked for only a little fruit, feeling like one of those diet-obsessed movie stars, but all I got in answer was roaring laughter.

"Fruit?"

Not more than a few minutes later, I watched as an entire quarter of grilled cow was thrown on the table. All right, now we're talking!

I ate like a primitive without either dishes or silverware, ending up with grease all over my hands and face. It tasted delicious!

"I bet you're wondering why our shop is so huge, aren't you?" asked Eitri.

"Actually...," I admitted.

"We need it to hold all the things we make and sometimes we make some very large things," he explained.

"And or course we can't accommodate the gods in a cramped space," continued Brokk.

"The gods... Do you mean to tell me that the gods come here, to your shop?" I asked surprised.

Brokk looked at me as if he had caught me spitting on the floor.

"What do you mean? Of course, they come here to pick up what they've asked us to make for them," he said, as if it were the most natural thing in the world.

"Especially Freyr and Odin," pointed out his brother.

On one of my normal mornings I ride my bike to school, stopping on the way at the Pieve Olimpia bakery to buy a snack, while at the same time two dwarfs are making stuff for Odin... After all, why should I think there was anything strange about that?

After the troll and the fire giant, all I needed were dwarves who were the gods' blacksmiths.

Was all this true, or was I ready to be locked up in an asylum?

I didn't know the answer to that question, but one thing I knew for sure was that it all seemed terribly real!

"I don't understand anything anymore," I snapped. "The village people are scared to death of an imaginary final battle among the gods and you're telling me that your works are ordered by Odin... But the gods don't exist!" I protested.

"That's not true at all," Eitri calmly replied. "The gods are real and come among us more than you might imagine."

"But that can't be... They are mythological characters, that's all."

"But didn't the Master explain anything to you?"

"Apart that in middle school we don't call our teachers master, who was supposed to explain anything to me? Our Italian teacher, or Ms. Bonelli?"

From the way the two dwarves looked at each other, I could see that I had just said something really dumb.

"We're talking about the Master who brought you all the way here."

"Actually, nobody brought me here. It was a stupid black sphere... Oh, I know, by any chance, do you mean Mr. Filippotti?"

"Filippotti? What a funny name he chose. Is he the guardian of one of the Spheres of Time?"

"Spheres... There's more than one?"

"Seven," stated Brokk.

"So where are they?" I asked.

"We don't know. The world has probably changed a lot since we have been living in the parallel crystal," added Brokk.

"What we do know is that one of the seven Spheres never stays in the same place. You might say it's a traveling Sphere," added his brother.

"So there are seven Spheres," I concluded.

"And each one is guarded by a Master of Knowledge."

"Well, that must be him," I confirmed.

"And he didn't tell you anything?"

"Actually, he told me about Superior Beings, about forces of nature and a lot of other things that I didn't really understand. A jumble of knowledge and information that confused me to say the least."

"But he must have told you that you're an Heir," said Brokk.

"Yes, he told me that. But how do you know?"

"We recognized you and, well, you're here...," noted Eitri, as if it were all rather obvious.

"You recognized me? How?"

"It's difficult to explain. Let's say we can sense it."

"It just keeps getting more complicated. But maybe you know how to help me get back and hopefully wake up from this weird dream."

"No, we don't know. Anyway, it's not a dream. You are really here in the flesh."

"Are you telling me I have to stay in this place forever?"

"No, you'll be able to get back because other Heirs before you have done it, only we don't know how. You'll probably figure it out for yourself."

"And in the meantime I've got to hang around here and put up with all these stories about gods and deities."

"You don't believe any of it, do you?"

"No, I've already told you. They're just myths that were once used to explain things like natural events, good and bad luck, good and bad harvests and so on. They're ancient beliefs from a time before most of these things were explained by science," I argued.

"This is the problem with all you mortals, you believe that a few hundred years can challenge immortality. As usual, mortals don't have any sense of perspective," Brokk said to his brother, who shrugged as if to say that was a given.

How come the dwarf had said... You mortals... As if... As if they weren't. The very thought made me gulp noisily.

"What do you mean, that...," but I didn't have the courage to finish the sentence.

Eitri said it for me. "That we are immortal? That's exactly what we mean. For once you've been able to figure something out."

"Immortal...," I managed to whisper.

"Immortal, yes, immortal, that's right. You know what it's like to live forever? To never die? Do you know what it's like to exist just as you are now, for all eternity?" Eitri asked me.

No, of course I didn't, but it didn't seem to be all that bad.

"Yet you look like you're a smart guy," persisted Brokk.

"Oh, thanks so much for the compliment."

"I didn't mean to offend you. But I thought that having met a troll and a fire giant might have helped you understand. I don't think you normally run into creatures like that in your world."

"No, that's for sure."

"You see then how insensitive it was of you to say that the gods are only myths, old stories to explain... What did you call them? Ah, yes, natural events, good and bad luck, etc. etc."

"So Ragnarok can't be the final battle of the gods otherwise everything would come to an end," I exclaimed.

"Ragnarok is a story made up by the gods so that mortals don't ever forget how strong and powerful the gods are. The gods have the power to destroy the world and then put it all back together again. People should be smart and never forget it."

"But the people in the village fear that Ragnarok is coming."

Brokk wagged his finger to indicate they were wrong. "In the past, we came close. The gods were angry with the people: between wars, famines and epidemics, humanity as you know it, was heading for extinction. Then the gods changed their minds. However, it doesn't mean that every now and then they won't fight each other."

"You know, sometimes they just get bored and want something to do, at other times they become quarrelsome and then..."

We heard a clap of thunder so powerful that the earth shook beneath our feet.

"They're fighting," said Brokk.

"What are they fighting about?"

"Any excuse is good. Could be over a bad joke, or someone wants something that belongs to someone else... As I said, any excuse is good," explained Eitri.

"Then there's always someone who isn't happy with the job he or she was given, so they try to take by force the job they believe is rightfully theirs," added Brokk.

"That's why they say "the gods are fickle," I said.

"More or less. That phrase was originally used in reference to different gods, the Greek gods to be exact, but I think it's appropriate in our current situation," agreed Eitri.

"Do you know the Greek gods?" I asked with astonishment.

"We've heard about them and other gods, too. That's all. Our own gods are more than enough for us."

More thunders.

"After all this talking, there's still something I haven't figured out."

"And what's that?"

"Where are we?"

"We are in one of the parallel crystals, the crystal of Yggdrasil," Brokk said.

"Stop, stop," I cried. "What? A crystal?"

"Obviously, your Master of Knowledge wasn't much of a teacher. We should really let him know," Brokk said to his brother.

"Yet he seemed really well prepared when we met him at the 300th Meeting of the Masters."

"Maybe he didn't have time."

"Maybe, but he certainly shouldn't allow the Heirs to go around so unprepared."

"Listen, listen to me. Mr. Filippotti explained everything. It's my fault. I'm a poor student and I have a hard time figuring things out," I said, trying to defend Mr. Filippotti.

"No need to make up excuses for him, but don't worry, we won't have him punished for it. Anyway... How can we explain... Of course the Masters are better at teaching these things, but I'll try," Brokk continued. "The crystals are parallel worlds that, at a certain point, detached themselves from the primary time flow and they... They became, crystallized, so to speak. Basically, the life in each crystal remains constantly rotating in the same age cycle."

"You sure are complicated," I exclaimed. "Let's see if I understand. The primary time keeps flowing and we are now in the year 2015. Right?"

"It's already 2015? Time sure does fly," said Eitri.

"At some point, an era of time gets disconnected from the primary time flow and eventually becomes its own world, where life remains crystallized in that specific period of time. Although the passing of time continues in the parallel crystal, it's like it's forever stuck in the same era. Sort of a closed community in which everything remains the same forever. Right?"

"That's about right. I guess my lesson wasn't too bad," said Brokk.

"But how is it possible for a world to become separated from the flow of time?"

"It's something the gods decide."

"So Odin and friends at some point decided that it was time to crystallize their world."

"Exactly," replied Eitri, applauding with his tiny hands.

"And how many crystals exist in addition to Yggdrasil?" I asked.

"We know of at least four others, but there are certainly many more."

"You mean to tell me you've never met people from the other crystals? I bet you have some wild parties among immortals," I teased them.

Eitri looked at me as though I had just made a raspberry in front of the school principal. "It is prohibited and very dangerous, and we can't go back to the primary time, either. Only the Heirs are able to do it."

I had just learned that I had been given a great privilege, I just didn't know what to do with it.

SIX
A STRANGE FISHERMAN

All through the night, bolts of lightning slashed the sky, followed by roaring claps of thunder. Sudden bursts of rain poured down like waterfalls. I had never in all my life seen such a huge quantity of water falling from the sky all at once. I tried to rest on the bedding thoughtfully provided by the dwarves, but it was practically impossible. I kept thinking about all the things I had learned over the past few hours, but I still couldn't believe all of it was true.

Fickle gods, parallel crystals, immortal dwarves... And all the rest.

How on earth had I ended up in this mess?

I was an Heir.

Yeah, but it wasn't my idea. Someone had made the decision for me without even asking my permission.

I wondered if my parents knew what was going on. Who knows, maybe they had always known about it and had kept me in the dark until I found out on my own. In that case, they could have at least warned me that sooner or later my life was going to be turned upside down.

That way I would have been more prepared for what had happened to me.

But I still didn't know what being an Heir was supposed to mean. I had the gift of being able to read animals' minds, and I could communicate my thoughts to them, too. I also understood the language of the Vikings as if I had spoken it all my life, but I couldn't see what good it would do me.

Who would care, anyway? When my mother was looking through the help wanted ads in the paper, I had never heard her say: "You need to know Norse for this job."

Yeah, right!

Oh, there was one other thing I could do: travel to all the parallel crystals.

Well, now, how could I make use of that?

I dunno!

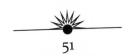

But there was one thing I knew for sure. I had to start looking for a way of getting back to Pieve Olimpia. I had no intention of spending the rest of my life wandering around the crystal of Yggdrasil.

What's more, the two dwarves did their best to stop me from getting any sleep and generally make the night a whole lot worse for me. They took turns sleeping.

While one of them slept, the other kept going from one window to another, as if they were expecting somebody.

Oh yeah, let me give you a tip, never sleep in the company of dwarves. They may be small but they snore like giants. In the end, despite everything, I finally managed to fall asleep.

When I woke up the next morning, I found myself alone in the house.

I got up. I was hungry. The huge hunk of meat was still on the table.

We hadn't been able to eat it most of it. I braced myself before tearing off a few pieces of the meat that had long gone cold and I ate it. It was still better than milk gone bad.

I went out. The sky was an iron gray color, but the rain had stopped.

I went down to the stream and washed my face in the freezing water. I was instantly awake. Then I walked over to the blacksmith shop.

"I've made up my mind. I've got to go find a way home," I announced. The two dwarves were completely absorbed in their work of forging iron.

Brokk was busy with the bellows while Eitri was skillfully using his slender hands to hammer the metal into shape.

They put down their tools and walked up to me.

"We knew you were going to make that decision. It's right that you should want to go home," said Brokk.

"It's just that I don't know which way to go. Have you got any suggestions?"

"We don't know and we wouldn't want to send you in the wrong direction. Don't worry, I'm sure you'll find the path you're looking for," said Brokk.

"Here, I made this for you."

Eitri handed me a ring. He had etched this symbol into it ᚺᚾᛁᛈ. I was about to ask what it meant, but... Wait a minute, I could understand the writing. He had written the word, Protection.

"But..."

"Runic alphabet," said Eitri, anticipating my question.

"I know how to read it without ever having seen it before. But how... How is that possible? Oh, I see. It's one of my abilities, one of my talents."

I put the ring on my index finger. It was a perfect fit. Eitri had made it without ever measuring my finger.

"It might come in handy," said the dwarf.

I stared at the ring wondering what powers it might be hiding, but I didn't dare ask. I was afraid of having to listen to another crazy story.

I thanked them and left. When I reached the stream I stopped, trying to figure out which way to go. I didn't see anything, no signal or board with a sign saying, "This way." If I'd had a coin in my pocket I would have tossed it, heads or tails.

Meow.

"Timoteo! Where have you been?"

He rubbed up against my legs. I bent down to pet him and he started purring in return.

"Ah, you've been hanging out in the woods... Well, you missed a great treat of barbecued meat."

Meanwhile, I had made my decision: I was going to go right.

I set off.

But Timoteo wasn't following me. He just sat and looked at me.

"What are you looking at? Come on, let's go."

His answer was to go off in the opposite direction.

"This way, come on."

Nothing doing, he just ignored me. He always did what he wanted.

At first I hesitated, then I decided to follow him, hoping that he wouldn't lead me to more trouble.

I had been walking for ages without meeting a soul, either mortal or immortal, and I began to get a little jittery. How could there not be anybody around here?

Surprisingly, Timoteo didn't wander off but stayed with me the whole way. Every now and then he would run ahead and perch himself up on a branch or a rock, waiting for me to reach him.

We walked along a well-marked trail that seemed to be traced out like a road, winding in and out of the woods. We still hadn't seen any sign of life. Not a village, not a hut, not a single thing to indicate the presence of a living creature.

I glanced at my watch. It still showed the time from when I had put my hands on the Sphere of Time. The strange thing was that the second hand was moving but the minute hand had stopped.

Maybe my watch was broken.

Suddenly, I heard the unmistakable noise of running water.

Whether it was a stream or a river, I'd soon find out. I had run into quite a few of them along the way.

I decided that I would stop and rest. I needed to soak my feet in the cold water for a while. Maybe, if I was lucky enough, I'd even manage to catch a fish. I was getting a little hungry.

"Hey, Timoteo, we're going to stop for a while," I told him, but the cat had disappeared.

"Timoteo, Timoteo," I called.

He had left me again. I wasn't going to worry about it anymore. I knew that when I least expected it, he would reappear.

As I approached the stream, I noticed something on the bank. It was a man sitting on a rock. I wondered what he might turn out to be: a monster, a god, a fantastic animal, or something else?

I approached cautiously, realizing the man had noticed I was there. He turned around and smiled at me.

He was an old man, with an old hat like those worn by fishermen. He wore a tunic similar to those owned by Mr. Filippotti and had leather sandals on his feet. The old man was dressed in a pretty weird way, to say the least.

He was holding a gnarly staff, made out of a tree branch.

He must have been blind in one eye because he had a bandage

over one of them.

He didn't seem to be hostile, so I threw caution to the wind and carefully approached him.

I sat on the bank of the stream and took off my sneakers, letting off a pretty disgusting smell. It felt so good to put my feet in the refreshing water.

"Young stranger, where are you going?" the old man asked me.

Seeing there was no one else there, obviously he was talking me. Just the same, I turned to face him and asked if he meant me.

"Do you see anyone else here?"

"No, but…"

"You don't want to answer my question?"

"No, I mean yes, but… I mean it's hard, and…," I babbled confused.

Good question: where I was going? Answer: wish I knew!

Since I had left the dwarves' place, I hadn't discovered anything to help me find my way back home. And how was I going to explain that to him?

"Speak freely, I know who you are," the man said as if reading my mind.

"And who are you?" I asked.

"My name is Vegetamr," he replied.

"Wanderer," I translated without thinking. From the way he was looking at me, it seemed he had expected a different reaction. He didn't get one. Was his name supposed to mean something to me?

"What do you know about the gods of Yggdrasil?" he then asked.

"Actually, not much. Our lessons on Viking history doesn't include the gods and if it wasn't for Ms. Bonelli, I'd know even less. She's a really cool teacher. She likes to tell us about things that aren't part of the study program so we can expand our knowledge."

"Bonelli," he mused as if the name reminded him of something.

"I know more about the gods of Ancient Egypt and Greece. We start learning about them in grade school."

"Enough, say no more," he said throwing his hands up with a disgusted look on his face.

"Well, I do know that Odin is the most important Viking god,

then there's Thor and the other gods and they all live in Asgard."

"That's more like it, but there's still lots more you need to learn."

He told me about the other gods. Loki, the god of deviousness and chaos, was an ingenious shape shifter and an evil deceiver. Then there was Hel, the goddess of death, who rules the underworld. And of course, he talked about Thor, the son of Odin and god of thunder, and his mighty hammer Mjollnir. He told me about many other gods, too, but after a while I asked him to stop because it had become too confusing.

"Don't worry, you won't forget any of the things I just told you," he said.

"I wouldn't be so sure. I've already forgotten about... Ouch!" I yelled. The ring Eitri had given me had suddenly become fiery hot. I couldn't get it off so I stuck my hand in the water.

The old man smiled.

"What's so funny," I snapped, "My finger was about to go up in flames," I exclaimed.

He burst out laughing. "Take your finger out of the water. It won't burn anymore."

I obeyed. It was true, the ring wasn't hot anymore. I looked at it and... There was a new word written in the runic alphabet: ᚺᚱᛈᛁ.

"Heir," I translated. "How did you... The inscription...," I was confused.

"This will help you to remember my lessons."

"But you... You..."

"Don't worry, you'll find your way back, but first you'll have to face some trials. The things I taught you will help you overcome the challenges."

"Trials? What sort of trials? "

"You'll find out soon enough."

"When will I know? I mean, I'd really like to get back home as soon as possible. I think my parents are waiting for me and I don't want them to worry."

He smiled again. "All in good time. Now I have to go."

He got up and gave me a basket of fish that had appeared out of nowhere.

"Are you a fisherman..."

Next, he handed me a branch. A bright flame burst out from one end.

"Don't let it go out if you want to cook the fish."

I grabbed the branch, holding it firmly, but I had to move quickly to protect the flame from a sudden gust of wind.

"Hey," I protested.

A gray horse was approaching from the sky. It was twice the size of a normal horse and it had... It had eight legs!

Vegetamr sprang onto the horse's back. The old man was unexpectedly nimble for someone his age.

"Let's go, Sleipnir," he thundered.

Sleipnir, Odin's horse.

Could it be that...

With a leap the horse flew up towards the sky. I watched as he went galloping away through the clouds.

So... So...

A shiver ran up my spine.

Vegetamr was none other than the mighty Odin.

SEVEN
MY ELF GUIDE

The gods do exist.

At this point, I was sure of it.

I had met and spoken with Odin. I saw him mount Sleipnir and ride up and away through the clouds.

Pretty hard to believe, isn't it?

Well, you'd better believe it because it's exactly what happened.

I know, I know, someone's probably thinking my imagination is galloping away just like that fantastic horse. A few of you are going to think I've seen Thor in 3D too many times.

But, I promise, it's all true!

Anyway, I only saw Thor once at the movies in Pieve Olimpia and it wasn't even a first run!

Well, anyway, think whatever you want, but it's all true.

And let me tell you, it wasn't the only time I met Odin.

You don't believe me?

Then just keep reading about the rest of my adventures in the parallel crystal of Yggdrasil.

By the way, after I had met Odin I also learned that Yggdrasil is the name of the cosmic tree in Norse religion.

Feeling stuffed from eating too much scorched fish and exhausted from all the walking I had done that day, I stretched out on the grass under the tree where I had stopped to rest. Lulled by the gurgling sound of the nearby stream, I fell asleep.

A short while later, I was awoken by a noise coming from the branches above me.

At first, I thought it was Timoteo who had decided to come back. But it wasn't.

I saw a boy perched on a branch above my head. He was watching me.

I sprang to my feet.

"It was about time you woke up," he said, nimbly jumping down.

He was a little shorter than me and I realized he didn't look like any kid I knew. In fact, he wasn't a kid at all. He had silver colored hair and slightly pointy ears. He was wearing a loose shirt over a pair of breeches. He had a bow slung over his shoulder and instead of a backpack, he carried a quiver with several arrows in it.

"Don't you know it's dangerous to sleep outdoors without shelter or protection, when there are trolls and giants around?" he chided.

"I guess you're right, but I was really tired and..."

"I'm Skap and I'm one of the Liosalfar," he introduced himself.

He had such a high-pitched voice, it sounded like he was squeaking. "Liosalfar are the elves of light that stand against the Døkkalfar, the elves of darkness that live underground and in the darkest forests," he explained.

"I'm Aki," I said, though I figured he probably already knew my name.

"I have been ordered to be your guide," he said.

"And who..."

He pointed to the sky.

"The powerful..."

"None other."

"Odin has ordered you to be my guide?" I asked, just to make sure I had understood.

"Let's just say that the order came from very high up."

"And where are you supposed to guide me?"

"I was told that you have a mission to accomplish."

"As far as I know, it was supposed to be a trial."

"Trial or mission, what's the difference?"

"Well, I think there's a big difference. A mission sounds like it's far more dangerous."

"Don't believe it. Some trials are so hard you end up risking your life."

"Well, thanks for making me feel better."

"Don't mention it. So, where do we have to go?"

"You're asking me?"

"It's your miss... Your trial."

"But I don't know anything about it," I protested.

"Well, I guess we'll have to find out, won't we? But if you keep hanging around here sleeping, we'll never get anywhere."

"Well, I'm awake now," I snapped.

"Good, then let's move."

I quickly pulled on my sneakers and went after him.

Skap walked rapidly. It seemed like his feet didn't even touch the ground. He didn't leave footprints where he walked, either, like his body was weightless.

"You're an Heir, right?"

"Yes, I guess," I replied tentatively. It was still hard for me to realize that I wasn't the same, regular kid I used to be.

"You Heirs don't often come to our crystal."

"How many have there been before me?" I asked.

"I wouldn't know because I'm usually not assigned to be a guide for you guys."

"And did they all go back? To the primary time, I mean."

He hesitated. "Why did you choose to come to our crystal?" he asked, instead of answering my question.

"I didn't choose a thing. I don't know why anyone would actually choose to come here. This is just where I happened to end up. If you must know the truth, I would have preferred not to come here at all. I would rather have stayed in the primary time," I replied.

He slowed down. "What's it like? The primary time world, I mean," he asked curiously.

"Well, it's different to this one. Very different," I replied.

It wasn't all that easy trying to find the right words to describe our era to someone who had missed out on a thousand years or so of evolution.

"To begin with, if we were in my era, we would be traveling by car or riding a bike instead of walking," I began. Of course, he just stared at me, totally baffled.

And that was just the beginning.

I tried to explain that our cities were built of concrete and asphalt, that instead of hunting for food we shopped at the grocery store, and that people dressed more or less like me.

"We don't need to find a stream for our drinking water or to

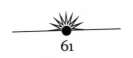

wash. Water comes through the faucets of our homes that are built of cement and bricks."

I also told him that our homes had heating and electricity that was used for a lot of different things.

"I didn't understand most of what you said, but I can see you have a lot of new stuff. Do all these new inventions make your life happier?" he asked.

"Well, for the most part, I'd say they do. But don't believe that it's all good," I added, telling him about air and water pollution and about trash.

Skap frowned at me. "I couldn't live in a place like that," he declared. "We elves need nature, clean air. And forests."

"It's not like they're all gone. It's just that there's not as many as there used to be," I ventured.

"You know what? I'm not all that interested anymore in seeing what life is like in the primary time."

"You mean, if you wanted to, you could travel..."

"No, it's impossible for me to travel, you know that. I was just saying."

We reached a crossroads. Without hesitating, Skap took the road to the right.

I realized I hadn't seen Timoteo for hours and it was beginning to worry me.

I had been hoping that he was following us and that he would suddenly jump out of nowhere, as he usually did.

"Where are we going? You seem to know exactly which road to take," I remarked.

"Since you don't know what's supposed to happen to you, I'm taking you to see someone who can tell us. We'll be there momentarily."

We walked down the trail until Skap announced, "we're here."

About twenty yards away, sheltered under the canopy of a huge ash tree, sat three women. The tree was so tall I couldn't see all the way to the top.

As we approached, I was overcome by strange visions. At first, the women appeared to me as happy, young girls. I lowered my head and when I looked up again, I saw three old women. Again I lowered my head, then looked up to find they had turned back into young girls.

This kept happening over and over until we reached the women. I raised and lowered my head a couple of times, but they had finally stopped transforming. The three women in front of me were about the same age as my history teacher. But they were less youthful looking, maybe because they didn't wear makeup and their clothes were not in the latest style. Their gray hair was tied back with ribbons of various colors: red, yellow and blue.

The women were working on a gigantic loom, weaving the biggest tapestry I had ever seen. I was sure there couldn't be a wall anywhere big enough for this tapestry to hang on.

"These women are the Norns," whispered Skap, who took a few steps towards them and bowed.

"Lovely and kind ladies, we have come here in your presence to know the fate that awaits this young Heir, who has traveled to our crystal," he said. At these words I stood and bowed like Skap had done. However, I wasn't really sure I wanted to know the answer to that question.

The three women smiled with amusement as they continued to weave the thread through the loom.

"Dear Liosalfar, this young man was not born on our crystal, so we don't have the thread of his life," replied the Norn wearing the red ribbon.

"Yes, I know, but I was wondering if there was a way to find out whose thread his path crosses."

The woman began to carefully study the tapestry. "You're asking me a very difficult question and I do not know if I can give you an answer, and...," she said, lowering her face right over the yarn. "Here, I've found your thread," she told Skap, "And... Yes, I see the presence of this young man on it. So, I see that you..."

Skap interrupted her. "Dear lady, don't worry about reading the ending."

"Are you sure?"

"Yes, yes, thank you."

"As you wish, but it might be better if you knew. Anyway, the young Heir..."

"Oh no, the thread broke," cried the Norn with the yellow ribbon, interrupting the Norn reading Skap's thread.

"Be careful," warned the third Norn.

"These things can happen, and after all, he was a seriously injured warrior," the Norn with the yellow ribbon defended herself.

"Be careful you don't let it happen with anyone else. This is the third person today whose life you have cut short," chided the Norn with the blue ribbon.

I looked at Skap and gulped. The fate of humans was written in those threads and it didn't take much to...

"It's hard to follow his trail," the Norn with the red ribbon continued, as she traced an invisible path on the loom with her finger. "Here, I found it again... On divine Freyja's thread, then here on Brisingamen's thread... Here it is... And..."

The Norn abruptly stopped without finishing her sentence, like she had suddenly lost her voice.

She snatched her finger from the loom as if she had burned herself. The Norn peered at me, making me feel uncomfortable. The other two Norns were also silent and gazed at me with worried expressions.

"Is there... Is something wrong?" Skap stammered.

"Hel," the Norn with the red ribbon said gravely.

Skap almost jumped out of his skin.

I knew who she was because Odin had told me. Hel was the goddess of the Underworld.

EIGHT
THE TRUTH ABOUT TIMOTEO

It seemed like the Norns had decided I was in for a nice little trip to the underworld.

And doesn't everybody go there at least once in their lives? All you have to do is find the right travel agency and... Presto, you're off, destination Underworld. Your travel package includes a meeting with the landlord and an organized tour through the flames. Important: remember to bring your burn lotion.

Joking aside, there really wasn't much to laugh about.

Mr. Filippotti had said that traveling with the Sphere of Time might be dangerous, but I had no idea the infernal abyss was on the list of possible dangers.

"I wouldn't want to be in your place," declared Skap.

"Would you just shut up, please? Ever since we left the Norns, you keep repeating that. I get it, OK? And thank you so much for the encouragement," I huffed.

"I'm sorry, I didn't mean to."

"I told you it's OK. But maybe there's something else you can explain to me. The Norn mentioned two other names. I know Freyja is the goddess of love, but who is Brisingamen?" I asked.

"Not who is it, but what is," he corrected me.

"It's a thing? What a name!"

"Yes, it's Freyja's magnificent necklace."

"Oh, I see," I said.

"This precious jewel has a certain story... How can I say this, the story is... Well, it's a little awkward," he said, whispering the last words.

"Why are you whispering?"

"Because it has to do with...," he breathed, pointing to the sky.

"Odin?"

"Hush. Yes, him too. He doesn't like to be reminded of what happened."

"Come on, tell me."

He looked around before speaking. "The goddess Freyja met four dwarves who were forging a fabulous jewel. When Freyja asked them for the necklace, the dwarves agreed to give it to her if she would spend the night with them. Freyja accepted the pact and so the jewel became hers. Loki found out what had happened and told Freyja's husband, Odur, who totally freaked out. He told Loki to bring him evidence to prove that it was true. Loki knew perfectly well that he couldn't just walk into Freyja's home, so he snuck in while she slept. Loki transformed himself into a fly and managed to steal the jewel. Once Odur had the evidence, hurt and saddened, he left for an unknown destination. When Freyja woke up and realized that both her husband and the necklace were gone, she knew immediately what had happened. So she decided to go to Odin to confess. Let me tell you, the father of the gods sure didn't take it very well. He was really upset and angry with Freyja for her appalling behavior. In the end, Odin forgave the goddess, but imposed a severe punishment on her. Freyja had to spend all eternity roaming all over the world to look for Odur, while wearing the necklace and crying the whole time over the loss of her husband" explained Skap.

While he was talking, Skap kept throwing furtive glances at the sky, afraid of being instantly struck down by a bolt of lightning.

"Wow, what a story!" I exclaimed.

"That's for sure... But don't go round babbling about it."

"OK, but what's the necklace got to do with me and Hel?"

He scratched his head. "How should I know?"

Couldn't those guys up there have sent me a better guide?

Meanwhile, another day was over and I was still stuck in the crystal of Yggdrasil, not knowing how to get back home.

We found a place to spend the night.

Skap offered me some beef jerky. It was a bit stringy, but it didn't taste all that bad.

"What a beautiful starry sky," he said, gazing up above. "Is it this beautiful in your era, too?"

"Yes, the stars are still there, it's just that it's not always easy to see them."

"Why not? Do you mean to say that even the sky is... What was

that word you used... I know, polluted. Even the sky's polluted?" he asked.

Sadly, I had to say it was.

"No way... Absolutely no way I would want to live in the primary time," he asserted with disgust.

A rustling sound in the grass announced the arrival of Timoteo.

"Hey, it's great to see you again. Where have you been all this time?"

I was sitting on the ground when Timoteo jumped into my arms, purring like crazy. I stroked him but he wouldn't calm down. In fact, he turned his yellow eyes on Skap and started growling. Then he hissed at the elf.

"What's going on?" I asked.

"Maybe it's better if you...," Skap started, as he climbed nimbly up the nearby tree, perching himself on a branch.

"Hey, Timoteo!" I exclaimed. "Calm down, buddy," I tried soothing him, but there was no way to get him to obey me.

He jumped under the branch and continued growling at the elf.

Timoteo was furious. I knew he wasn't an easy cat to deal with, but I had never seen him like that.

"Go away," screamed Skap, but the cat just hissed at him even more furiously. Timoteo flattened his ears and let out a low, menacing growl as he continued to spot the elf.

By reading Timoteo's mind, I managed to discover the reason he was so aggressive.

He knew who Skap was and I could see why there was bad blood between the two.

It wasn't easy, but I finally managed to calm down the cat and took him up in my arms.

"Isn't there something you need to tell me?" I asked Skap.

"I don't like cats."

"Looks like the feeling is mutual. But that's not what I meant."

"What, then?" he asked, but I could tell from the way he said it that he knew exactly what I meant.

"About the Heir who came here before me."

"I don't know what you're talking about," he lied.

"Timoteo told me."

"What, is he a talking cat?"

"No, but you should know that I can read animals' minds."
Silence.

"Well?" I urged.

"If I come down, will he attack me?"

"No, he won't," I said, although I'm not sure Timoteo actually agreed with me.

Reluctantly, Skap came down from the tree, but kept his distance. "I don't want to get a piece of his claws," he said.

"He won't scratch you," I reassured him.

However, Timoteo's thoughts were not very comforting.

"Calm down, calm down, buddy," I murmured, stroking his thick fur. I could feel him starting to relax and finally he began to purr.

Skap approached cautiously and sat down on the grass in front of me. He kept the bow and quiver within his grasp. But if Timoteo had decided to jump at him, the elf would never have had enough time to nock an arrow.

"First of all, explain to me how you know each other."

"If I had known that horrible cat was with you, I would have refused to be your guide. However, a refusal would not have been taken very well by the guys upstairs."

"When did the two of you meet?"

He thought about it. "According to the calculations used in the primary time, I would say four years ago."

"Timoteo had already been here four years ago?" I asked surprised.

"Well, I don't think it was his first time here."

"How... How is this possible? Timoteo would've been at the most two or three years old," I protested.

"So what?"

"But how..."

He looked at me as if he didn't understand what I meant. "So, why do you think it's strange?"

"But, it's... It's impossible!"

"Not for the Gaia spirits," he said.

"What spirits?" I asked in astonishment. I suddenly had the feeling I was about to be told another incredible story!

"Gaia spirits, the spirits of Mother Earth from the primary time," he explained, like it were something everybody knew about.

"Wait, wait a minute. Are you telling me that this flesh and bones cat that I'm holding in my arms is a spirit?"

"Well, not exactly. So this is how it works, let's say the cat is the wrapping, or the container of the Gaia spirit that is inside him."

I stopped stroking Timoteo and looked at him like he was some creature I had never seen before. Actually, he was. He wasn't really the normal cat I had thought him to be. "I wish at least I knew what Gaia spirits are."

Skap grimaced in realizing my total ignorance regarding spirits. "I told you, they're spirits of Mother Earth. You humans don't understand that the Earth is not only a planet, but it's also a living organism that gives and sustains life. The Earth produces a lot of energies that sometimes take the form of spirits that live within the body of other living creatures."

"And then what happens?" I urged him.

"And then they remain in that body, at least until they're forced to find another one."

"What do you mean?"

"The energy of the spirits is strong and has lots of different effects on the host body."

"What kind of effects?"

"See the cat? When the spirit entered Timoteo, his body was reinvigorated. He became immune to all diseases and he grows old at a much slower rate than a normal cat."

"So how old is Timoteo?"

"Who knows? You said he was three, but he might be ten or twenty times older than that. As long as the spirit remains in his body, you'll hardly notice he's getting older. But once his body has been worn out by time, the spirit will leave and then his end will come very quickly."

"But why do the Gaia spirits accompany Heirs?"

"Their strong bond with the earth will help get you back home."

Now I understood why Mr. Filippotti had told me never to get separated from Timoteo. He was my return ticket to Pieve Olimpia. However, first I had to find the way to get back, and I still didn't know where it was.

"What happened to the other Heir who came here with Timoteo? Why does he hate you so much?"

"Well... It's kind of an unfortunate thing," he said, obviously embarrassed. "You see, it was only my first assignment," he tried to justify himself.

"What assignment, exactly?"

"I was supposed to guide an Heir who was searching for the way back to the primary time."

"The same assignment you were given for me, so that means you know where we have to go."

"Oh, no. It changes all the time."

"So, what happened?"

He looked down. "It didn't go well," he admitted, bowing his head. "The Heir wasn't able to get back," he said.

"He's still here?"

"Yes."

I got goose bumps. I had never thought that I might end up having to stay in the crystal of Yggdrasil.

"We had found the passage and we were almost there, when suddenly Fenrir, the wolf, came up behind us. The cat was running up front, then came the Heir and I was last," he said. "I got scared," he whimpered. "I should have slowed the wolf down, but instead I just fled. The cat managed to get into the passage, but the Heir didn't make it and ended up in the jaws of the beast."

"The wolf, Fenrir, is a really huge animal," I observed.

"Yes."

"What a horrible way to go."

"I'm so sorry," he whispered.

"Now I understand why Timoteo is so angry at you. You didn't protect the Heir and Timoteo came back alone."

Not only didn't the Heir make it back, he got mauled by a giant wolf. Stuff to make you wet yourself, just thinking about it.

"I won't get another chance."

"After my, you mean?"

"Yes. If I fail, the Liosalfar will kick me out and I'll end up in the darkness with the Døkkalfar."

"Don't even think about it," I cried.

NINE
A Fierce Battle

I woke up as the dawn colors were lighting up the sky. I had fallen asleep with Timoteo next to me, but he wasn't there anymore. Skap was sitting on a tree branch above my head.

"You finally woke up," he said and hopped down from the tree.

"Where's Timoteo?" I asked him. Now, more than ever, I wanted the cat to stay with me.

He shrugged. "He's gone."

"I can see that for myself," I snapped. "Couldn't you stop him from leaving?"

"Who, me? Didn't you see how he was hissing at me? I certainly didn't want to get scratched. But don't worry, he'll be back."

"I sure hope so."

"Come on, let's get going...," began Skap, but stopped abruptly.

"Where..."

"Hush," he silenced me, holding a finger up to his lips so I would keep quiet.

He concentrated, listening to something. I couldn't hear anything, apart from the usual sounds of the forest.

"Can't you hear it?" he asked.

"Hear what? I can't hear anything."

"There, listen."

Nothing.

"Did you hear it?"

I shook my head.

"Again. You hear it now?"

Nothing. Evidently, super hearing was not one of my powers as Heir.

"Nope."

"This time you must have..."

"Yes, I heard it," I exclaimed. "A noise like... Like an explosion."

"And not only. There's a battle going on," he declared, without any doubt.

"Are you sure?"

"Yes. Let's go see."

"Is it absolutely necessary?" I asked, but Skap had already set off at his normal rapid pace.

Judging by the way he moved even faster than usual, he must have been in a hurry to get to the scene of the battle. A couple of times I had to stop because I was out of breath.

Why all the hurry?

After all, it's not like we were going to a party or something.

As we got closer, the sounds became clearer: screams and battle cries, horses whinnying, the clang of weapons clashing, metal against metal, and then thunderous blasts.

A real battle!

I thought of all those times when sitting in front of my computer I had identified with the hero in my video games. But this was all for real. I started to get a bit uneasy.

"Come on, let's move," urged Skap.

As we climbed up the slope, it seemed that the noises were gradually fading.

"Sounds like it's all over," said the elf, clearly disappointment.

Finally, we reached the top of the hill. Below us there was a vast plain where I could see that the battle, at this point, was almost over.

The scene in front of me was... It was unbelievable, scary, crazy, horrifying and any other description you can think of after I tell you what I saw. The plain was littered with the dead and wounded, alongside broken shields and smashed helmets, broken swords and dented armor.

The first thing that got my attention was the sight of two fire giants leaving the scene.

The blasts I had heard were the sounds of their deadly fireballs. I couldn't stand to think of the horrible fate of the poor guys who had been hit by the fireballs. I could see there had been raging fires in several places on the battlefield.

Next, I saw some trolls, like the one I had previously met, who were running off in the opposite direction to the giants. I counted

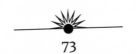

about a dozen of them, all huge and scary. A seriously injured, badly burned troll was still fighting against a handful of men determined to finish him off with swords and axes. His desperate cries sounded like mooing, but a hundred times louder.

And then there were the humans. Two Viking armies had faced off in a fierce battle with axes, swords, hammers and spears, leaving numerous victims on the battlefield.

It was so gruesome I really don't want to describe it. Too horrible to talk about.

"It's all over," said Skap.

He was looking over the battlefield, too, but didn't seem to be as upset by the horror as I was. I figured that clashes like that happened often enough in the crystal of Yggdrasil.

"It's terrible," was all I could say.

"Wars are never pleasant, wherever they are fought," observed Skap, turning his head as if he had noticed something and...

"Get down!" he yelled, pushing me to the ground.

A moment later, a giant winged monster flew right over our heads, barely missing us. But the monster caused a gust of wind that rolled us along the grass like soccer balls.

"Nidhogg!" exclaimed Skap.

It was an enormous dragon with wings like a prehistoric bird, horns like an elk and feet with long, sharp claws.

The dragon flew down onto the plain like a bomber pilot and hurled fire-bombs at the enemy line. We watched as the dragon used its mighty talons to grab the injured troll by the shoulders, lifting him like a twig. He flew straight up to the gray skies, almost out of sight, then swooped down and slammed the troll against a rocky ridge. The impact jarred the earth like an earthquake.

Nidhogg let out a shrill victory cry before hurling more flames on his enemies, defeating the last few who were still resisting. The dragon shot back up and sped off like a rocket.

"Hel sent her winged dragon," remarked Skap.

"You mean... That huge monster comes from the underworld?" I asked.

"In Hel's kingdom, he torments the dead and feeds on them."

What kind of monsters lurked in the underworld, I wondered?

By now I was hoping and praying that the Norns' prophecy was totally wrong.

If I had to face Hel, I would never come out alive. No, no, there had to be another way to find the way back to Pieve Olimpia.

"Come on, let's go down to the plain. I want to see who fought against Hel's army," said Skap. We started down the slope until we reached the plain.

The smell was horrible, beyond description. It was a mix of burning flesh, acrid smoke and trash rotting in the sun. I don't know how I managed to not throw up.

Flocks of crows swooped down on the battlefield, their sharp beaks wreaking havoc on the bodies already mangled by the weapons.

"Let's go back," I pleaded.

I couldn't stay in that place of death a minute longer.

"Hold on," said Skap as he looked around hoping to find something, maybe a symbol or a sign to help him figure out which god had challenged the formidable Hel.

Unexpectedly, I ended up helping him.

Many women and children had come to take care of the remains of a loved one who had not survived the battle.

Not far away, I recognized Gerrid bent over the body of a warrior, and Karli was next to her. I was afraid that Bjarni had perished in battle and unfortunately he had.

I walked slowly towards them, hoping they wouldn't blame me for what had happened. I remembered very well how I had been forced to flee the village.

"Karli," I called out when I was a few feet away from him.

He turned towards me. I could see he was trying to hold back the tears but without success. Gerrid turned around, too. Her stern, grim face was fixed in a stone mask. She wouldn't shed a tear, not on the battlefield, at least.

"I'm sorry," I whispered.

Bjarni was dead. His many wounds were proof of how valiantly he had fought.

I was afraid that Gerrid would drive me away, but I was surprised by her reaction.

"It wasn't Ragnarok. It was not your fault, young traveler."

"But I saw... I saw the fire giants and...," I began.

"It has nothing to do with you. The gods are quarreling. They were fighting among themselves."

"It sounded like it was something pretty serious."

"I don't know. Soon after you left, the divine Freyr arrived at our village riding his golden boar. He asked our warriors to join his army in the fight against the evil Loki."

Meanwhile, Skap had come up behind me. "But we saw Nidhogg," he joined in.

"We saw it, too, as well as the fire giants. Loki didn't fight alone. His daughter, the fearsome Hel, sent some of her messengers of death."

"Loki and Freyr... Freyr and Loki...," brooded the elf, scratching his pointy ears.

"I am very sorry for Bjarni," I said and hugged Karli who put his head on my shoulder and wept. I was choking up and had to swallow several times to drive back my tears.

"Karli," Gerrid called him to her.

He pulled away from me, sniffed loudly and wiped his eyes on his tunic sleeve.

"I'm leaving now," I said.

Just then a trail of light shot across the dark sky. It looked like a ray of sunshine when it cuts through the clouds. Except this trail was milky white and wrapped in a haze that shimmered like it was made of billions of rhinestones.

I gasped. Seven horses with riders had appeared on the luminous trail. Women armed with lance and shield were riding down the trail of white light.

"The Valkyries," announced Skap.

Wow, they sure were beautiful. The most beautiful women I had ever seen in my life. They had long blond hair framing perfect faces and were wearing leather breastplates. They moved with such lightness and grace that they seemed to float through the air.

I thought such beauty could only be a vision, but it wasn't!

They moved along the trail of light and then rode across the plain, coming to a stop right in front of us. They dismounted. They were tall and walked with graceful movements as if they were models walking down the catwalk at a fashion show. They were gorgeous!

My face was on fire and I felt a strange tingling all over. My heart was beating so loudly it sounded like a heavy metal concert.

"We came for Bjarni," said a Valkyrie. Her voice was like a soft caress.

My jaw dropped and one of them smiled at me as she ruffled my hair, making me blush.

I was embarrassing myself!

Gerrid knelt and let the Valkyries take hold of her husband's body. He was a huge man, yet they lifted him easily. After laying him over one of the horses, they began to get back in their saddles.

"Bjarni will fight in Odin's army," said another Valkyrie.

A woman came up running. "Please, please take my husband," she cried.

But when she got closer, the Valkyries pointed their lances at her.

"Your husband was not brave. His fate lies elsewhere. Go away."

Without another word, they mounted their horses and rode along the luminous trail. When they were far away, the light disappeared and the sky became a compact mass of clouds again.

"Hey, wake up," said Skap, nudging me under the chin.

"The Valkyries," I whispered.

"They always have this effect on Heirs. Haven't you ever seen women on horseback?"

"Oh, sure... I mean no... I mean they're so... Gorgeous."

"Yes, certainly, but they're gone now. Now you can come back down to earth."

"They've taken Bjarni."

"Sure, he was a brave warrior and now he'll become an einherjar. Odin will need heroic warriors in his army when Ragnarok comes for real," he explained.

77

But why did I have to end up right in Hel's kingdom? Couldn't I have been lucky enough to the where the Valkyries dwell? Nah, my usual bad luck!

TEN
MY INSANE MISSION

"I don't understand. I just don't understand why Freyr and Loki would want to fight against each other," Skap kept repeating.

We had left the site of the battle ages ago and for all that time he had done nothing but ask the same question over and over.

"OK, so Loki likes to brawl and he can be pretty darn hateful, but Freyr... Freyr is the god of beauty, he's a god of peace and serenity. Why would he want to fight Loki?" he kept saying.

I listened without saying a word. I didn't know anything about it and anyway, all I wanted to think about was the vision of the fabulous Valkyries.

Still, one thing was pretty clear to me. When the gods fight it's the people who pay the price, with men fighting and dying in battle in the name of the gods.

"What if his sister Freyja was the cause," Skap wondered.

I let him ramble on as I walked in silence, remembering how good the Valkyrie's touch felt when she ruffled my hair.

"I think I know," Skap suddenly exclaimed.

"Really?" I asked distractedly. I can't say I was all that interested.

"So, I've already told you the story about Freyja and the role Loki had in it, right?"

"Yes, you told me that story."

"Clearly, those two don't like each other very much. Maybe the goddess asked her brother to help her get back at Loki."

"Now? After all this time?"

"Well, they don't think like mortals from the primary time. For the gods, measuring time doesn't make any sense. They're immortal, so the passing of time is all very relative."

"So they love, hate or whatever each other, forever."

"More or less."

"What a difficult life they have."

"Well, it's not like just anyone can become a god."

"That's true. But not everyone would want to be a god either. I

don't think I'd like to be one."

"But there are also many advantages."

"Maybe, but I prefer to be exactly what I am. If you want to know the truth, the only thing I want right now is to find a way of getting back to Pieve Olimpia. We're just walking around aimlessly and it seems like we're wasting our... My time."

But Skap wasn't even listening to me. He was still trying to figure out what was going on with the gods. "But if that were the case, then why not get help from the god Heimdall? He is the guardian of the gods and has already won a battle against Loki. That time it was to rescue Freyja, too," Skap rambled on.

"Skap... Skaaap, are you listening to me?"

"Yes, yes, that is... I was thinking that the connection must once again be Brisingamen. Old grudges never go away."

"You've already made that clear."

"And whose destiny crosses paths with the jewel?"

"How would I know!"

"What do you mean, you don't know... Don't you remember what the Norns said? It's your destiny!"

"What's that supposed to mean?"

"That it wasn't a coincidence that we witnessed the battle between Freyr and Loki."

"Oh, really? And what's the connection?"

"Yes, well, the connection is... Just like I told you, it's the necklace."

"Why?"

"Well, because... Let me think about it and I bet I can find an explanation."

"Go for it. Meanwhile, are we going to keep heading in this direction?" I asked as we reached a fork in the path.

"Whichever direction you want."

"What do you mean, where I want to go? You're the one who's supposed to be the guide," I reminded him.

He scratched his silvery hair. "Well then, we'll go this way."

With a guide like that, I was afraid we'd end up in the underworld without even knowing it. And it would not be a pleasant surprise.

"Odin, couldn't you have sent me a better guide?" I said under my breath, looking skyward. The ring vibrated on my finger like I had been pinched and it made me jump.

Was it possible that the mighty Odin had heard me?

A little further on, we sat down to rest on the trunk of a fallen tree. My feet and legs were hurting. In the past few days I had done nothing but walk, walk and walk.

Actually, sometimes I had also been forced to run.

To go where?

I dunno!

Just then Timoteo made his appearance and I happily picked him up and hugged him. He purred contentedly, and snuggled into my arms.

I hadn't seen him around lately, but I was certain he had never lost sight of me. He was a real guide, unlike Skap.

"Will you tell me where we're going?" I asked the elf. "We're wasting time," I added, rather annoyed.

"I don't like your tone."

Clearly, he was upset.

"Oh, really? So answer me. Where are we going?" I insisted.

"We're looking for the passage to the primary time world."

"Thanks, I could have told you that. But we don't seem to be making much progress."

Timoteo was suddenly watchful. With his senses on full alert, he seemed to catch something that our ears couldn't hear.

"What's up?" I asked.

A strange noise, something or someone approaching.

He jumped to the ground and ran off into the tall grass, disappearing from view.

"Timoteo," I called him, but it was too late. "See you later," I said crestfallen.

"Skap, get ready. We're about to have a visitor," I told him, a little worried. Was it better to wait or run away as fast as our legs could carry us?

I hadn't even finished speaking when an incredible scene materialized before my eyes. I saw a carriage that looked like a

Roman chariot being pulled by two cats. It was driven by a woman who glimmered like her clothes were made of gold. They were coming down an invisible path over the treetops.

"It's Freyja!" exclaimed Skap.

For a moment, the chariot disappeared from view only to reappear, slowly losing altitude until it landed just a couple of yards away from us.

Skap had literally prostrated himself on the ground. I wasn't quite sure how to welcome a goddess, so to avoid making mistakes, I knelt on one knee. But I hadn't been able to take my eyes off that glittering apparition.

The cats came to halt a few steps away from me and calmly sat down, like pulling the carriage hadn't taken any effort at all. Sure, they were two big, strapping cats, one ginger and the other gray, probably of Norwegian breed. But even if they were a bit bigger and stronger than Timoteo, it seemed impossible that they could pull such a weight. It certainly couldn't have happened in a "normal" world, anyway. On the other hand, in the world of the gods it seemed anything was possible.

I tried to read the minds of the two cats, but I succeeded only in part. It was like there was interference, like when you're trying to get a radio station and it doesn't work right away and the voices are interrupted by buzzing noises.

Freyja got off her carriage and came towards me. I felt myself wrapped in a wind like a fresh sea breeze on a summer's night.

"Get up," she said. Her voice was gentle and commanding at the same time.

I looked up at her. She was as beautiful as a Valkyrie, except her hair was the color of copper. She glowed with a golden light that was so intense I wished I had my sunglasses.

"Do you know who I am?" she asked me.

Freyja was gorgeous and although she looked at me with motherly reassuring kindness, my legs were shaking.

"You're... You are the goddess Freyja," I replied hesitantly. I tried to seem more confident and bold, but I couldn't manage it.

Don't think it's all that easy to talk to a god, because even just

being in their presence is intimidating. I don't quite know how to explain it.

It could be due to the aura of energy that surrounds them, or because suddenly you can feel a tension in the air. Or maybe it's the thought that the person in front of you is immortal. Whatever the reason, you get like a strange tingling. It runs from the back of your neck down to your knees that immediately begin to shake. You even feel like your teeth will start to chatter, as if you're freezing to death.

That's what it's like, that's how you feel.

The goddess smiled in hearing my answer. "And you're an Heir. What a coincidence, you're just who I need," she said. I couldn't begin to imagine how I could help her.

"Oh, really?" I stammered.

"I have to entrust you with a mission," she said, causing the tingling down my back to become annoyingly stronger. Meanwhile, Skap had found the courage to get up and came to my side.

"What can I do for you?" I asked, wondering if I had been rude in speaking like that to a goddess. Maybe I should have said, 'my lady' or something. Or 'your divinity' might have been better.

Who knows, but she didn't seem annoyed, so I figured I hadn't made a total mess of it.

"First, I have to ask you if you will accept it."

"I don't think I have any choice. The great Odin told me I will have to go through some trials before I can return to the world of the primary time. But I'd really like to know something about it."

"The greatest difficulty is always in the details."

"To me it seems like more than just a detail, but..."

"There's a bit of tension among the gods at this time," she began.

"I figured that much. Freyr and Loki faced off in a tough battle."

"Right," she confirmed bitterly," and, as usual, Loki played dirty."

"We saw Nidhogg," Skap interrupted.

"Without Hel's help, I don't know how it would have ended. As I was saying, there's tension because something precious was taken from me: my necklace."

"Yesss, I knew it, I knew it," yelled Skap, like he had guessed the winning lotto combination.

Freyja looked at him sternly and I was afraid she was going to instantly incinerate him. Skap noticed and threw himself like a doormat at her feet.

While Skap was there, one of cats decided he might as well nibble the tip of the elf's ear.

"Ouch," he yelled, shielding his ears with his hands. One thing was for sure, he didn't have a good relationship with cats.

"My Brisingamen necklace was stolen. See this?" she said, leaning toward me. Around her queenly throat you could see a lighter colored band of skin that hadn't tanned, apparently because she used to wear a necklace. I drew closer and saw that the band of skin pulsed with a myriad of flashing dots like, when your TV loses the signal.

"Er... I see," I agreed, feeling embarrassed because my nose was two inches from her skin. I could smell her perfume, but couldn't figure out what the fragrance was. It seemed like a mix of roses, lavender and vanilla. Anyway, whatever it was, I really liked it and I wondered if that was the scent of the gods.

"I need you to help me get it back."

"But how?"

"I'm convinced that Loki is the culprit, but he says it wasn't him. I believe he's lying."

"And how am I supposed to..."

"Wait, I haven't finished. Loki loaded two fallen warriors on his giant serpent, Jormugand, and together they rode to the entrance of Hel's kingdom. Loki waited there for the warriors to enter. I think he gave one of them my necklace, so now it must be hidden in his wicked daughter's kingdom."

"And...?"

"You have to help me recover it."

"So I need to enter Hel's kingdom," I concluded.

"Exactly."

"Excuse me, divine Freyja, but why don't you, together with Thor, Odin and your brother, burst right in there and get it back?" I asked naively.

"None of us can invade the territory of another god. That's the

84

rule."

"You guys are so complicated," I barely whispered.

"Did you say something?"

"Er... No, nothing," I answered. I felt my face burning. I must have turned red as a beetroot.

"Then you'll do it?"

"But why me? There are many brave warriors who surely have a greater chance of success. I'm only twelve..."

I whimpered.

"Only the dead may enter Hel's kingdom. Nobody else can get in and..."

"But I'm alive!" I protested, interrupting her.

"Let me finish. Because you're an Heir, you can travel in the parallel crystals and you have the power to enter every dimension within each crystal, from the celestial spaces to the darkest abyss of the underworld," she explained.

Well, then. Now I had discovered I had another power that was of no use to me. Freyja talked about it as if it were a huge privilege, but I sure didn't feel that way. To tell you the truth, I would rather not have anything to do with something like that.

"So you're asking me to accept the mission of getting Brisingamen back from the underworld. Right?"

"That's right."

I felt my stomach churning.

What choice did I have?

Refuse to do it and I would have to stay forever in the crystal of Yggdrasil, or accept and get a pass to go back home to Pieve Olimpia.

Well, if these were my only two options, it would be a no brainer, but there was another possible outcome that scared me to death: I might descend into the underworld and never come back out.

Was I exaggerating to think such a thing?

I sure don't think so. A run-in with the goddess of the underworld was not something that should be taken lightly.

"Can I count on you, Aki?" the goddess asked me. She even knew my name.

"Okay," I said without giving it any more thought. I immediately regretted it, but it was too late.

"Great. You won't be alone on your trip to Hel's kingdom, and..."

"Yes, Skap will be with me," I interrupted her again. I seemed to have this bad habit of interrupting the gods.

"Oh, I didn't mean him. Not only him, anyway," she continued, looking sideways at the elf still lying at her feet, and still trying to fend off the cats. "You can get up," she said, kicking him lightly with the tip of her divine toe.

"Who then?" I asked.

She stretched her arms in front of me and turned her palms toward the ground. A column of light came up from the grass until it reached her hands. It looked like a mini hurricane with billions of golden dust particles swirling in a vortex. Then the little whirlwind subsided and before my eyes the particles became compact, until they took the form of a girl. I gasped. Better than any magic trick I've ever seen. In that moment I was reminded of some famous magicians and illusionists who would have died of envy.

"This is Gersemi, my daughter."

I would have figured it even if she hadn't told me. The resemblance was truly remarkable. Gersemi looked like a miniature of her mother.

"Very pleased to meet you, Gersemi. I'm Aki," I introduced myself.

Very pleased? What was I thinking? Couldn't I come up with something better to say? You can really tell that females make me feel uncomfortable. I sure had made a fool of myself. The gods really bewilder me. So do their kids.

"She will accompany you on your journey. Good luck, young Heir," she said, getting ready to leave. "See you soon. I hope."

Then she grabbed the reins of her chariot and the cats rose up to the sky, and took off along the invisible path.

ELEVEN
RIDING ON A FLYING CHARIOT

Gersemi was my age. Actually, what I mean is, she looked my age but she'd been like that forever, or almost forever. A god doesn't age and is immortal. And that's true for the children of the gods, too. I haven't figured out if they're born the way they are, or if at some point they stop growing. Anyway, I know that's the way they stay forever. Eternal children, eternal adolescents. I bet there are people in the primary time world who wouldn't mind that at all.

I've got to admit that, at first, I wasn't all that happy to have the daughter of a goddess as my travel buddy. I imagined her to be spoiled, squeamish and snobbish, like certain pretty girls from Pieve Olimpia, but I was wrong. She was lively and cheerful and very, very curious. She wanted to know a whole lot of things about girls my age in the primary time world. What they wore, how they talked, how they behaved, and even how they flirted. I wasn't exactly an expert on the subject, so it wasn't an easy task. Trying to explain how girls keep in touch by texting on their smartphones, or describing low-rise jeans was harder than any math quiz I've ever taken.

She listened attentively and memorized everything without any problems, even words that she had never heard before and were impossible to translate into Old Norse. She said she would have loved to wear new clothes like the ones I had described, but she wasn't allowed to. She was forced to wear a long white robe and a light cloak that seemed woven with gold thread, pinned to her shoulders. She added that she would like to change her hairstyle, too, but that wasn't allowed either. Gersemi had to wear her long, copper colored hair loose over her shoulders and tied back to her head by a thin, golden ribbon.

"My sister Hnoss is luckier than me. She has a head full of blond curls and can change her hairstyle however she wants," explained Gersemi.

I listened, but didn't ask why her sister could do it and she couldn't. I guess that even though she was the daughter of a goddess, Gersemi was not that different from the "normal" girls I knew. But when she got tired of walking she revealed her true self. In fact, Gersemi could vanish in a cloud of gold dust before my very eyes and reappear whenever she felt like it.

Anyway, after the encounter with the divine Freyja I had no doubts what my destination was: the realm of the goddess Hel. I had assumed that Skap would know which direction to take, but instead he looked puzzled and undecided. When I asked him why, he explained that although he knew which way to go, he didn't actually know where to find the entry to the underworld. There were not many who knew, he told me, and Gersemi confirmed it.

"Hel's kingdom is over there," stated the elf, indicating an indefinite point somewhere in front of us.

"At least we know in which direction we need to go. Then when we get there, we'll ask someone," I said, but they stared at me as if I had stolen the coins from the offering plate at church.

"It's dangerous. If we go the wrong way we may never be able to find the gates to the underworld and we risk wandering around for all eternity," explained Skap.

"So what do we do?"

"Let's get going, we'll decide on the way," said Gersemi, taking the initiative.

I wanted to ask if she couldn't go to her mother for help, but thought better of it.

We headed down the trail but had walked only a few steps when a maroon squirrel flew past us going two hundred miles an hour.

"Ratatoskr!" Skap and Gersemi cried out in unison.

A split second later, a huge gray cat streaked past us at the speed of lightning, chasing after the squirrel. "Timoteo!" I exclaimed.

We looked at one another.

"Who is Ratatoskr?" I asked.

"Who is Timoteo?" Gersemi wanted to know.

It was Skap who answered both questions. "Timoteo is the spirit of Gaia Aki," he said, "and Ratatoskr is the only creature that knows every nook and cranny of Yggdrasil. It's because he travels tirelessly all over the crystal, from one extreme to another, from Asgard to Hel. He's a kind of messenger."

"So the squirrel would be able to tell us...," but I couldn't finish my sentence because Skap and Gersemi had thrown themselves in pursuit of the squirrel.

I followed them, struggling to keep from laughing. Just imagine the scene: a squirrel that went flying down the trail like a Ferrari, followed by a cat racing along to stay at his heels. Then came a pointy-eared elf that ran with short, swift steps without leaving footprints and finally, the daughter of a goddess who seemed to glide along the ground like she was on a surfboard. If I hadn't seen it with my own eyes, I would've thought it was one of the most ridiculous stories I'd ever heard.

Anyway, Timoteo was the only one who managed to keep up with the squirrel. Skap couldn't manage that crazy fast pace for long, and I came panting up to him with my tongue hanging out. Gersemi preferred to disappear in a golden cloud rather than show herself defeated by a squirrel.

"Anyway, he'll have to come back this way," panted Skap.

"Are you sure?" I asked out of breath.

"Yes, I told you. Ratatoskr travels continuously all over the crystal, from Asgard to Hel, two of the nine realms of Yggdrasil."

"Nine?"

"You know only about Asgard, where the gods live, and Hel, the underworld, but there are seven more."

He told me their names. Midgard, the world of men, is in the middle of Yggdrasil. Muspellheim, halfway between Asgard and Hel, is a world that blazes and burns, where the fire giants live. There are five other kingdoms populated by monsters and giants, whose names are too hard to remember or to spell.

We resumed our journey until we reached Timoteo. He had lost the squirrel, too and stared ahead gloomily.

"It's OK, don't worry," I told him. "He's too fast for you, too."

He replied with a meow. He agreed. I realized that he had never seen a rodent that could run so fast.

Meanwhile, the weather had changed. A damp fog had lifted and the air had become cooler. The sweatshirt I was wearing wasn't warm enough and I was full of inch high goose bumps. The sky had become so dark that it was the color of blacktop.

"Maybe we should try to find shelter and wait out this nasty weather," I suggested.

Among other things, we were forced to walk slowly because the visibility had become so bad.

"We'll wait forever, then. We just entered the darkest part of the crystal. It's always like this here."

"What a sad place," I shuddered.

"May I remind you that we're getting closer to the underworld? What did you expect to find?"

"You're right."

A sudden glow announced the return of Gersemi. "Excuse me, but I was busy," she told us, as a way of explaining why she had left us on our own for so long.

"Oh, don't worry, we managed. Apart from losing sight of the squirrel, nothing else happened," I said, but Gersemi didn't seem to appreciate my joke.

Anyway, I wasn't the only one bothered by that horrible weather and black sky. Skap didn't say a word and looked concerned.

"This weather puts you in a bad mood, too, doesn't it?" I asked him.

"I wish that was all that's bothering me."

"Why, what's wrong?"

"We just walked into Svartalfheim," he said. Svartalfheim was the kingdom of the Døkkalfar, the elves of darkness.

Our bleak and gloomy surroundings kept getting worse as we penetrated deeper into the realm of the elves of darkness. The vegetation on both sides of the trail all but disappeared and the land turned into an ash-like gray. The trees were bare, with strangely shaped skeletal trunks and twisted branches that looked like long claws. Real scary scenery. Skap was nervous and kept turning his head back and forth like he was at a tennis match.

"Cold and dark, cold and dark... That's not my thing," he kept repeating, almost whimpering.

"Look, if you really must know, I don't want to stay in this crystal either, so help me get home and it will be better for both of us," I said.

I hadn't forgotten that our fates were tied to one another; if I returned to Pieve Olimpia, he would avoid having to live with the Døkkalfar. Otherwise... No, better not to think about it.

"Right, right," he said, but then started moaning again.

The bleakness of Svartalfheim had made Gersemi gloomy, too, as she walked ahead of us without saying a word. I hurried to catch up to her.

"Nasty place, huh?" I quipped, just for something to say.

She turned and looked at me as if seeing me for the first time. Clearly, she had other things on her mind. "What? Yeah, sure. Nasty place," she repeated without much enthusiasm.

Actually, she didn't seem all that upset by the eerie landscape around us. I wondered if she had already been here and knew what to expect or maybe, as a daughter of the gods, it wouldn't look good if she seemed upset, like it would have been bad manners or something.

"It's freezing, too," I continued, rubbing my hands.

"Yes, it's freezing, too," she repeated after me.

You could tell she didn't really want to talk with me, so she would probably just repeat anything I said to her. She wasn't all that nice after all, I thought. We walked in silence while I scanned that bleak landscape looking for Timoteo, but I didn't see him. He was really good at following me while remaining hidden.

"Aki," called Gersemi. I walked up beside her again.

"Sorry for before."

"For what?" I asked.

"I didn't feel like talking."

"Yes, I figured as much."

"I wasn't upset with you. I had a fight with my mother," she confessed.

"Sorry," I said, not knowing what to say as I tried to imagine how an argument would go between a goddess and her children.

I wonder if instead of a spanking they let fly with thunder and lightning. She shrugged.

"Before, when I left, I didn't mean to abandon you. I went to my mother to ask for her help to find Hel, but she didn't want to," Gersemi explained.

"She wants us to do everything on our own, right?"

"Yes, but it's also my fault."

"Why's that?"

"It's my punishment for fighting with my sister, Hnoss," she answered.

For a regular kid, punishment was a day with no video games. For the daughter of a goddess, punishment meant having to come down from Asgard to hang out with some totally boring mortals, while looking for the door to the underworld. I was reminded of Giulio, who often ended up getting caught in the middle of fights between his sisters. After all, girls were the same everywhere and they weren't any different just because their parents were gods. Not that any of this would have made Giulio feel any better.

"Don't worry, we'll make it," I said, although I wasn't so sure we would.

Gersemi smiled. A beautiful smile, worthy of a goddess. I could feel my cheeks burning. As we walked along side by side, she told me about the really strict education of young people, the children of the gods. Each one was assigned a god as instructor that had to teach them many things, including the history of Yggdrasil and the nine realms, particularly the realm of Asgard and the gods who lived there. Since the gods were immortal, I figured their history must have been practically infinite. Most of all, I kept thinking what torture it must be to have to go to school all your life, a life that went on forever.

"I was assigned Skadi, the goddess of the mountains and hunting, and of the cold and frost. I think she's a good teacher, it's just that her palace Thrymheimr, where the lessons are held, is always freezing."

She was telling me that Thor's son, Magni, was one of her companions, when we heard a commotion behind us.

"Help!" cried Skap.

While we were chatting, we hadn't realized that the elves of darkness had us surrounded. I couldn't say how many there were. A lot for sure, but it was hard to count them because they were difficult to see in the dark. Unlike the elves of light, the Døkkalfar were dressed in pitch black. They were hairless and had hooked noses, but the most disturbing thing was their eyes, because the whites were dark gray and the pupil was red. They were small in stature and as agile as gazelles. Some of them had assaulted Skap, who was trying to free himself from their grip.

"Let me go," he yelled.

Although we were surrounded, the elves didn't look as if they were going to attack us. I figured they recognized Gersemi.

"What are you doing in our kingdom?" one of them asked. He had a raspy voice.

"We're just passing through. We're on our way to Hel's kingdom," said Gersemi.

"Ah, the underworld. And why did no one bother to tell us that the Freyja's daughter would be passing through our kingdom along with... With... Who are you, anyway?" he asked me.

He got in my face. He barely came up to my belly button; he may have been small, but he sure looked menacing. He smelled of wet ash. "I'm..."

"He's a friend of mine," said Gersemi.

"A friend... And where does this friend of yours come from?" he asked suspiciously.

He was very interested in my clothes and grabbed the sleeve of my sweatshirt with his bony hands.

"From a long way away."

Meanwhile, his little hand was squeezing my arm and it hurt.

"Hey, let me go," I yelled.

I tried to yank my arm away, but I couldn't get him off me.

"Interesting," continued the elf.

They didn't seem willing to let us go and things weren't looking good.

"Let us go," ordered Gersemi.

Skap was in trouble. He could no longer hold off the elves of darkness that surrounded him.

"Let you go? You can leave. We would never want to make the divine Freyja angry. However, your friends will stay with us for a while."

A dozen elves were closing the circle around us. At that moment Gersemi dissolved into a golden glow and disappeared. Thanks for sneaking off, I thought to myself. But Gersemi reappeared outside of the circle and with a charge worthy of a football linebacker, made a few of the elves tumble to the ground. I took advantage of the situation. I grabbed the elf that was holding my arm and pushed him against some of his friends.

Then I rushed over to help Skap. Unfortunately, the surprise didn't last long and in no time the elves regrouped and were back on the attack. Just then, a golden trail pierced the fog and darkness. We all turned as Freyja's chariot appeared, pulled by the cats but without a driver. Gersemi disappeared to reappear on the chariot with the reins in her hand. As she passed over my head, I leaped up and managed to grab hold. I was left dangling for a bit before being able to pull myself into the chariot. I sat beside Gersemi as she made a U-turn and with a reckless maneuver at low altitude, flew towards Skap. I leaned forward and managed to grab his hands. The elves bombarded us with rocks, but missed.

With difficulty, I managed to get Skap on board, while Gersemi took off at great speed, making maneuvers worthy of a Blue Angels pilot.

"Hey, slow down a bit," I yelled.

"Are you crazy? My mother never lets me use her chariot. When will I ever get a chance like this again?"

TWELVE
WHAT YOU WOULD CALL A TOTAL DISASTER

It was amazing to see the two cats effortlessly dashing through the sky like they were running around on the lawn. They moved their legs at breakneck speed and pulled their ears back while using their tails as helms. Gersemi spurred them on, like a cowboy from the Old West on his galloping horse. She was bursting with happiness from every pore. She was totally thrilled.

"Come on, let's go!" she cried, grabbing the reins that were tied under the belly of the big cats.

We had been riding through the sky for quite a while when suddenly we began to lose altitude, like a plane that had run out of fuel.

"Come on you mangy cats, get back up there," Gersemi urged them, but obviously the cats were responding to another command because they soon touched down in a perfect landing and then stood still.

Gersemi tried to get them going again, but all she got was angry hissing and growls.

"They say we have to get off," I said after finally managing to read their thoughts between one bzz bzz and another.

Gersemi stared at me, until she remembered about my power.

"I bet it was my mother who ordered them to land."

"I'm pretty sure you're right."

"Well, at least we've left behind the realm of Svartalfheim," said a relieved Skap.

Once we were out of the chariot, it took off in the usual trail of light until it disappeared.

"In the end, your mother did help us," I noted.

Gersemi nodded. "If only she would have told me, there'd have been no need fight about it."

"Thank goodness, anyway! Who knows what ideas those horrible little creatures were coming up with," said Skap, as if he was a lot taller the other elves.

"How long will it take?" I wanted to know.

"Not long. In a little while we will be entering the realm of Hel, and we have to look for the gates."

"Is there anyone who can help us?"

"I'm sure that in Asgard there are many who know where we have to go. And then there is always Ratatoskr. If we manage to follow him for a while, maybe he'll lead us to the entrance of the underworld."

The route leading to Hel was bleak and dark, even more than Svartalfheim. The mist was rising in steamy wisps from the murky waters that smelled like sulfur. The air was so hot it felt like having a hair dryer pointed at your face. The few plants were reduced to burned and blackened bushes. No form of life could survive in this arid place. The sky was a solid, impenetrable black slab. At least it wasn't cold. Actually, as we went deeper into this desolate area the temperature kept rising.

I took off my sweatshirt and tied it around my waist.

"You guys were right." I said, "With all this fog, we risk getting lost in this awful place."

"I know," confirmed Skap, looking around fearfully.

Timoteo had shown up and was walking slowly along with us.

With so much fur, the heat must be unbearable. I wondered if the spirit of Gaia inside him was beginning to sweat as much as we were.

Gersemi didn't appear to be particularly affected by our surroundings and not even the heat seemed to bother her much. Maybe the gods didn't sweat?

Suddenly I saw Timoteo prick up his ears. He had sensed something.

"What's happening?" I asked him.

He communicated that he was sure Ratatoskr was approaching.

He could hear it and he was ready to throw himself in pursuit. Timoteo loved chasing the squirrel.

I had an idea. Pity I didn't think to share my idea with my fellow travelers. If I had, I would have avoided the disaster.

Ratatoskr appeared quite suddenly, flying out of the fog like a missile. Without giving it a second thought, I threw my sweatshirt at him. My aim was perfect and the squirrel ended up inside the hoody. He slowed his pace but didn't stop. I clung to the sweatshirt and, with unsuspected strength, the squirrel managed to drag me quite a way along the hard ground. Although I scraped my elbows, I hung in there until I managed to stop him.

I wrapped him completely inside the sweatshirt and held him tight while he struggled furiously. I never thought a squirrel could be so strong.

Timoteo was at my feet, wagging his tail. He had every intention of sharing in the prize.

"I'll let you go," I told the squirrel. "Just tell me where I can find the entrance to the underworld."

Ratatoskr filled me with insults that I had no problem understanding despite all the bzz bzz. In that moment I realized he was a special creature, like the cats that pulled Freyja's chariot.

However, I didn't let him go.

"I don't want to hurt you. I'd just like you to help me. I really need your help," I said.

More insults.

I didn't let him go even though I was really sorry that I had to keep him wrapped in my sweatshirt.

But eventually he gave up.

He began to give me directions when Gersemi and Skap sprang out from the fog.

Proud of myself, I welcomed them with a triumphant smile.

"Ratatoskr is giving me directions," I said.

"Ratatoskr?" asked Skap, while Gersemi raised a hand to her mouth.

I nodded.

"Ratatoskr... He's... He's in there?" he asked horrified, pointing to the sweatshirt.

I sensed that I had done something unforgivable.

"Yes," I said hesitantly.

"Let him go, now!" he ordered.

"But..."

"Now!" he repeated, clearly terrified.

I obeyed.

Leaping out of my sweatshirt, the squirrel launched more insults at me and sped off, fast as an arrow.

Timoteo couldn't wait to chase after him, only for the fun of it because he knew that he would never catch the squirrel.

"But... I don't understand. Why are you so worried? After all, I didn't hurt him and..."

At that moment, the black sky was slashed by a bolt of lightning that struck the ground right in front of us, creating a gorge hundreds of feet deep. The lightening was followed by thunder that was louder than any I had every heard. It made my ears ring for several minutes.

Next it began to hail, only instead of ice pellets, the sky dumped drops of molten lava on us.

"Let's get out of here," yelled Gersemi.

We ran after her, zigzagging in an attempt to avoid the drops of lava, until we found shelter under a rocky ridge.

"Just made it!" exclaimed Skap, as he extinguished a flame on his tunic caused by falling lava.

"What's happening?" I asked.

They frowned at me.

"You mean to say that it's... That it's because of Ratatoskr... That it's my fault for holding him back...," I stammered, but couldn't complete the sentence.

"Yeees!!!" they yelled at me together.

"I didn't know," I apologized, deeply sorry. "But how it is possible that a squirrel can..."

"Ratatoskr is one of nature's messengers. His constant coming and going from Asgard to Hel is proof that the chain of life in Yggdrasil isn't broken..." explained Gersemi.

"...That the gods of the heavens and those of the underworld are still fighting and there's no winner...," continued Skap.

"...That the circle of death and rebirth is not broken," added Gersemi.

"Do you understand now who Ratatoskr is? He wasn't the one who unleashed this uproar. What you did has angered all, and I mean every single one, of the forces of nature," concluded Skap.

I gulped noisily. I sure had made a big mess.

But I hadn't done it on purpose!

The incandescent rain suddenly stopped, but our troubles didn't. I didn't have time to breathe a sigh of relief before noticing, thanks to the light of the fires set by the lava, a winged creature fast approaching. It was huge!

"Nidhogg!" shrieked Skap.

We left the makeshift shelter a split second before the huge horned dragon spat flames at us. Gersemi vanished in a golden glow while Skap and I fled in search of another shelter.

The huge winged beast first flew skyward, then swooped down on us.

"Let's split up," I yelled at Skap, hoping we would confuse the beast. The plan worked, but only for a moment because the dragon flew back up then flung himself at me. I was the chosen victim. This time I had no hope of getting out of it. I was going to end up grilled like skewered meat at a Fourth of July cookout.

But once again, Gersemi came to my rescue.

Well, it wasn't actually Gersemi personally.

The black sky opened up and flooded me with a blinding light. A powerful figure emerged from the cone of light and threw itself on the dragon. I turned just in time to see a hammer come down hard on Nidhogg's head. Caught by surprise, the dragon decided to hightail it out of there instead of trying to fight back. With a few beats of his massive wings he disappeared, swallowed up by the darkness.

"Thor," whispered Skap, as the mighty god touched ground a few feet away from me.

Remember Arnold Schwarzenegger in Conan the Barbarian?

Well, multiply that by two and you'll get an idea of what the god Thor was like... Wow, Mr. Doldi should be proud of how I described all this.

He was over nine feet tall, with biceps the size of large barrels, a chest as big as a pool table and hands capable of crushing a basketball like a ping pong ball.

His long, blond hair tumbled out below the Viking helmet on his head. He was wearing a short tunic tied at the waist with a big leather belt. Thor's legs were like granite and the top of my head reached just below his... Well, you know. In one hand he was clutching his hammer, Mjollnir, whose head was a parallelepiped piece of granite the size of a small car. It was mounted on a short, stocky handle with a very elaborate pommel shaped like a man's head. Totally awesome!

Gersemi appeared at his side.

"Thanks," she said.

"You have to thank Magni. You're his favorite classmate," the god replied. His voice rumbled like distant thunder.

"Th-th-thank you S-S-Sir Thor," I stammered.

He leaned toward me, bending on one knee, as if he wanted to take a closer look at me. The finger he pointed at me was so powerful he could have flicked me away like an insect.

"Be careful next time. It is always better to stay away from anything that you do not understand," he admonished me, knowing very well who was the cause of this whole mess." Otherwise, you get yourself into trouble," he added.

He gave Gersemi a light pat on the cheek, then, with a huge bound, propelled himself up into the cone of light, until he passed through the dark clouds and disappeared from view.

After Thor's passage through the clouds, the sky closed up, turning back into a slab of pitch-black.

"I'm sorry," I said.

"This time we got lucky," said Skap, breathing a sigh of relief.

"Thanks to Gersemi," I pointed out.

"Let's just say thanks to my friends in Asgard," she corrected.

"The fact remains that without you we would have ended up in the clutches of the elves of darkness, or roasted by Nidhogg's flames."

"But that didn't happen."

"I'm sorry, I'm really sorry," I repeated.

"At least let's hope it was worth it. Did you find out which way we should go?"

I couldn't help grinning a bit. "Yes, Ratatoskr told me," I said.

THIRTEEN
Hanging Out in the Underworld

The directions I had forced out of Ratatoskr had proved accurate, and we arrived at the entrance to the underworld without running into any more obstacles. We stood before a gate several feet high that barred access to a deep, dark cave called Gnipahellir.

If you think that the Vikings' underworld is a hot, fiery place, you're wrong. Even as we were traveling down the last stretch of road, the temperature had dropped abruptly. When we arrived at the cave, we were struck by an icy wind. It was like someone had left a door open, leaving us in the middle of a strong air current.

"I'll freeze to death," I said with chattering teeth.

"Here, wear this," said Gersemi, handing me a coarse woolen tunic that appeared by magic in her hands.

I put it on, but still couldn't get warm.

"That's all the help I can give you. I'm sorry, but I can't go any further," she added.

I had figured she would leave us. The gods and their children were not permitted to pass through the gates to the kingdom of the lady of the underworld. Unwritten codes, but applied for all eternity.

"I guess I might as well go back with you. I don't have the keys to open that," I said pointing to the gate.

Famous last words. A hair-raising creaking heralded the opening of the gate as it slowly twisted on its hinges.

"I get the impression you're expected," whispered Skap.

"Well... So, do you think I should go?"

"I'll come with you!" exclaimed the elf.

"But you can't... It could be very dangerous. Elves can't...," he didn't let me finish.

"I've made my decision. After coming all this way, I have no intention of leaving you on your own," he declared.

That was really nice of Skap, although his company so far hadn't been much help. But I didn't say anything because I didn't want to offend him. However, it was very brave of the elf, because entering

Hel could prove fatal him.

"I'll wait for your return," Gersemi said reassuringly, to give us courage.

I sure didn't want to go through that gate, but what choice did I have? It was dangerous, but I had to do it if I wanted to get back to Pieve Olimpia.

My heart was thumping in my chest as I passed through the gate.

There was a light mist that stung my face like it was made of invisible pins. Millions of icicles were hanging from the cave's ceiling. An intense white light ahead of us prevented us from seeing what lay beyond.

We continued deeper into the cave until we were forced to stop.

The path narrowed and we joined a line of people.

Panic constricted my throat.

They weren't regular people, they were... They were all dead!

Empty eye sockets stared at us. Some of their faces had skin so transparent you could see through to the skull bones. Some coughed, others made a kind of muffled gasping sound. They were all wearing identical course, mousy colored robes.

They weren't scary, though. They didn't look at us menacingly, they just seemed very sad.

We heard a frightening noise that went echoing through the cave. It sounded like a dog barking, except it was as loud as the engine of a tractor.

"Garmr!" exclaimed Skap.

"Who is Garmr?"

"It's Hel's dog."

Must be a strange dog, I thought.

The line of people began to move again and we advanced a little. The barking noise had become so loud that it made the ground under our feet shake, but I still couldn't figure out where it was coming from. Garmr, or whatever it was, remained invisible.

We advanced a little further until the mist cleared and I saw him.

He was huge! He looked like a mastiff, but was twice the size of a rhinoceros. His short black fur was mottled with red patches. He was tied to a chain, like the ones that hold a ship's anchor, attached to the cave wall.

The dead were advancing towards him without any fear. They offered the dog something that he quickly swallowed, then they just kept on going as if the beast were only an image.

"What are they giving him?"

"It's sweet bread mixed with their own blood," said Skap.

Yuck!

Garmr sniffed the air, then barked so loudly that my teeth snapped.

"He smelled our scent. We're not dead," Skap said.

Not yet, I thought.

The giant dog growled and showed his fearsome jaws.

"How do we get by it?" I asked.

"We could try to get someone to give us a few pieces of bread. Maybe we can trick him," Skap ventured, but he didn't sound convinced.

It's impossible to fool a bloodhound's sense of smell.

I focused on his thoughts. It was a hard thing to do because of the interference caused by his "special animal" brain. However, seeing I had succeeded with a very angry Ratatoskr, I could probably do it with that big dog, too. It was absolutely vital that I succeed.

Meanwhile, the line was slowly advancing and now we had only a few people... Er, dead people in front of us.

"What do you think?" insisted Skap.

"Hush, don't distract me."

"Move!"

As Garmr swallowed the offerings he didn't take his eyes off us for even a moment. He stared at us menacingly. Now he could tell exactly where the strange smell was coming from.

The unfamiliar scent of living creatures.

We were next.

"Stay back," I whispered to Skap.

Then I stepped forward, pretending to be full of confidence.

I'd like to tell you that I confronted him without fear, but that would be an outright lie. Actually, I was afraid I was going to wet my pants.

I took a few steps and then I sat down and opened my arms as I had done with Maciste, the Filippi's vicious pit bull. I hoped it would work.

Garmr had never been petted in his whole long, immortal life. And that was a really, really long time.

The enormous dog growled and barked at me, slamming his stinky breath in face. It was like sticking my head out the window of a car going three hundred miles an hour through a landfill. I was literally drenched with flying spittle and pieces of sweet bread that stuck all over my face and hair.

It was totally gross!

I wiped my eyes on the sleeve of my tunic and the rough fabric scratched my face.

But I didn't move. I remained very still in front of him.

As he sniffed me, my face got slathered with his huge wet nose.

I reached out and stroked the fur on his bristly snout.

Garmr suddenly jumped back as if I had scared him, but then he came up to me again. I laid my hand on his giant head and patted him with a firm touch. He liked it. He lay on his stomach and began to wag his tail as he breathed through his mouth with his tongue lolling. Another wave of hot, stinky breath struck me.

I motioned Skap to go by and the elf slipped furtively around the dog. When he was at a safe distance, he began to run. He had made it. Now it was my turn.

Meanwhile, the dead people behind me were beginning to rumble because my improvised show was delaying their passage to the underworld.

"Dear Garmr, the people are getting impatient. Maybe it's better if we stop now," I suggested.

Someone in line came up with the bad idea of throwing a piece of fallen icicle at Garmr.

Garmr lunged and barked so loudly that it made the first few people in line tumble backwards like dried leaves blown by the wind.

"Let me go. I'll come back later," I told him.

Garmr yelped like a puppy and licked me with his course tongue.

I really needed a shower now.

Without turning back, I slowly walked off with my hands in my pockets, like I was strolling through downtown Pieve Olimpia.

I had managed to get by the guardian of Hel's kingdom. I couldn't believe it. If that was just the beginning, I wondered what else was in store for us. I reached Skap, who was waiting for me at the end of the cave.

He hugged me.

"I was afraid we would never make it. When I saw Garmr come up to you I shut my eyes... You know you're a bit smelly?"

"Thanks a lot. I can hear the sound of water... What's up ahead?" I asked.

"We've almost reached the Gjöll River."

"River? Great, I can wash myself," I said and set off quickly towards the riverbank.

"I think that at most you can rinse your face off. The water is freezing and it's not unusual for one of the dead people to fall into it," said Skap, but I didn't hear him because I was already gone.

I knelt on the bank and washed my face. It was like putting ice packs on it, but at least I got the dog's drool off me. I dipped my cupped hands into the water and...

"Ahhh!" I sprang back.

Pale white bones were floating towards the shore.

"You could've told me that..."

"I tried to warn you but you didn't hear me," retorted Skap.

"What is this stuff... I mean, who are they?"

"Let's keep going and you'll understand," he replied.

We resumed our journey to the goddess Hel's palace and joined the crowd that was approaching a sparkly bridge.

Skap explained that it was the golden bridge Gjallarbrú, where you crossed the river to reach Hel's palace.

And it was made of pure gold. Try to imagine a bridge built like an interstate overpass, except a bit narrower and without guardrails, with everything, absolutely everything, made of gold. If you scraped off a bit of gold dust with a box cutter, you would become very, very rich. Pity that all who managed to see it no longer had any use for gold, silver, money or any other sort of riches.

Crossing the bridge wasn't as easy as it might seem. You had to get by a female giant named Modgud, who guarded the access to the bridge. With her skeletal face and holding a huge sword, she decided which people would pass and which ones had to wait.

"Slow down, slow down! You're dead, so what's the hurry," she shrieked.

She could stop whomever she wanted from going across and anyone who became indignant got a backhanded slap that sent them into the river.

"This explains the bones in the river," I said.

"But she's not really allowed to. She can't stop the dead from crossing the river and presenting themselves to the goddess of the underworld," observed Skap.

"Why don't you tell her?"

"I don't want to go for a swim in the icy water." Modgud blocked a small group of the dearly departed.

"No, no, don't even think about it. You can't get through here," she said, shaking a finger at them the size of a baseball bat.

"You have to go that way," she added, pointing to a steep path that ran alongside the bridge.

Without protest, the people bowed their heads and changed direction.

"What about them?" I asked.

"Nasty people."

"Not that the rest of them are nice folks."

"They're murderers, adulterers and guilty of perjury. Destination: Nastrond."

"Nastrond?"

"Yes, it's a huge beach and their fate is to be plagued by a tangle of snakes and be eaten by Nidhogg."

"That's good to know. Let's stay away from that road. Come on," I prompted.

We shoved and kicked our way through the crowd until we reached Modgud. To the giant we probably looked no bigger than a Ken action figure.

"Slow down, there's no hurry, you're dead," she repeated, this time

with a big belly laugh.

"We're not dead," I shouted.

Suddenly there was total silence and thousands of empty sockets turned to look at me.

Modgud stuck her sword in the ice and knelt down to see me better.

"And who are you?"

"My name is Aki and I'm an Heir. I have to see the lady of this place," I replied with confidence.

"How did you manage to get by Garmr?"

"He's my friend."

"That mutt has no friends."

"Maybe that was true before. But he has one now."

"What do you want?"

"To get by. I have to meet with the goddess Hel. That's all."

"That's all," she mimicked. "Is he with you?" she asked, pointing to Skap, who was shaking like a leaf. His face was the color of egg white.

"Yes, he's with me."

"Elves and dwarves. Ugh!"

"He's with me," I repeated.

"He's not passing."

"He's with me," I said again, with determination.

"If he wants to go, he'll have to swim."

I tried to argue, but Modgud had made her decision. She gave me a shove and I found myself tumbling along the bridge, while the sound of a splash told me that Skap had been tossed into the water.

I got back up and leaned over the edge of the golden bridge.

Skap was floundering in the icy water.

I stretched as much as possible to try and grab him, but he was too far away.

I had to think of something.

There was a continuous flow of the dead. The journey towards the other side of the bridge was slow. But there was no way I could ask any of them to help me. However...

I tripped up one of them and he fell forward. He tried to get

up but only managed to move awkwardly, giving the impression of swimming in a pool without water.

I ripped his robe off him. His skin was as thin as tissue paper and you could see his bones like on an X-ray.

I slammed down another one of the dead and did the same thing to him, then knotted the two robes together and threw them over the edge.

"Grab it!" I shouted to Skap.

The elf fought to emerge from the water and managed to grab hold of the robe. However, even if he was small and skinny, he was still too heavy for me. I dug my heels in right at the edge of the bridge and tied one end of the robe around my waist.

"Move!" I yelled at him.

I was holding on as hard as I could, but soon I would have to give up. Just when I couldn't hold onto Skap any longer and was about to let go, his hand gripped the edge of the bridge. We had made it.

He was soaked. "Damn Modgud," he said, then spat out some of the water he had been drinking.

"Why does she hate you?"

"The giants can't stand dwarves and elves. They may be big and strong, but we're smarter and more agile and we often play tricks on them."

"Here, if you want, you can wear this," I said, untying the knot between the robes.

"No, thanks, I prefer to stay wet rather than wear that stuff."

I threw the robes back to their owners, who were still trying to get to their feet.

I waited while Skap caught his breath, then we headed down the last stretch of the bridge, until we were in sight of a square building with two towers on either side. It was as tall as a ten-story building and had dazzling white walls of ice. The doors, also made of ice, were flung open to welcome all those who had gotten by the fierce Garmr and the terrible Modgud, and were able to cross the golden bridge.

"Éljúðnir, the palace of the goddess Hel," said Skap.

FOURTEEN
IN THE PRESENCE OF THE GODDESS
OF THE UNDERWORLD

We walked through the doors of Eljúðnir.

I expected to enter a luxurious palace full of antiques, gold trim and shiny marble floors; after all, I was entering the palace of a goddess. Instead, it was nothing like that. The enormous lobby had nothing in it at all, not even a bench so you could rest after the long walk to get there.

At the far end of the lobby there were three doorways cloaked in mist.

Some of the dead people went through the one on the right, others through the one on the left. No one went through the icy doorway directly in front of us.

"Usually, those who get this far know where they will be spending the rest of eternity. The only ones who go through that middle door are those still waiting to learn their destination, or who want to appeal the decision," explained Skap.

"I see. I guess that's the one we should go through to meet the goddess," I concluded.

Skap nodded.

The lobby had a gloomy atmosphere and was immersed in a dense fog, making it look like someone had sent a huge barbecue up in smoke.

"Do you hear it, too?" I asked Skap.

I thought I could hear another sound mixed with the sorrowful murmuring of the dead. It was like a constant hissing noise, but I couldn't quite figure out what it was.

"I can't tell… All I hear is a constant buzzing," he answered. Well, thank goodness that he's the one with great hearing.

We went forward cautiously, as the fog gradually cleared and…

The walls… That's where the hissing was coming from. The walls were made of live snakes that…

"Stay down," I yelled at Skap, as we threw ourselves to the

ground between the legs of the dead who were advancing down the lobby, while the snakes spat streams of poison. We managed to avoid getting hit only because we were down on the ground.

"That was close," I said.

"That's for sure. Yuck, what a mess!" exclaimed Skap.

We hunched over and hurried as fast as we could, till we reached the doorway.

As we approached, I noticed the engravings depicting scenes of death and torture on the ice doors. They were accurate down to the tiniest, most disgusting detail.

"I've never visited at the home of a god. What are you supposed to do in these cases? Do you knock?" I asked.

"I don't know... Maybe it's already open and you just...," Skap said. He had barely leaned against the door when, very slowly, it opened.

The door scraped along the ice, making a sound like chalk on a blackboard going through a thousand watts amplifier.

We were greeted by the usual swirl of frosty air that froze my eyelids, when suddenly two individuals materialized in front of us.

"They're Hel's two servants, Ganglati and Ganglot," whispered Skap.

"Nice names!" I exclaimed.

In Old Norse, Ganglati means lazy, while Ganglot translates more or less as slob.

Their empty sockets probably meant they had been serving the queen of the underworld since time immemorial. Ganglati was tall and lanky and walked hunched over, dragging his feet. After every third word, he yawned. On the other hand, Ganglot was more petite. She lived up to her name by wearing clothes that were all torn and full of holes, and had black streaks on her cheeks. Her long hair was caked with dirt that had built up since the beginning of time.

"We are Ganglati and... yawn... Ganglot. Welcome, what can we do... yawn... yawn... For you."

I know you've already figured out who said that.

"We would like to see the lady of the palace," I said.

"As you can imagine... yawn... Given this crowd... yawn... She is very busy... yawn... So we'll have to ask her... yawn... If she has time for... yawn... You."

His laziness was contagious. Listening to him made you feel like putting on your PJs and getting into bed.

"Try asking her. I think she's expecting us," I said.

"You go, I'll... yawn... Wait here."

"Always me, always me. You never want to do anything," snapped Ganglot, before spitting on the floor. A real lady.

As she shuffled off, her feet left two dark tracks, like the marks left by car tires when you slam on the brakes.

We stood there waiting, while Ganglati took the opportunity to lean against a wall and take a nap. He fell asleep in that position and began to snore.

Luckily, we didn't have long to wait.

"Come, come on in," shouted Ganglot, in a voice as shrill as a crow.

"Mr. Ganglati, sorry to bother you, but will you come with us?" He opened an empty eye socket. "Just go... yawn... That way." "Okay. Take it easy."

We found Ganglot by following the dirt marks she had left.

"The lady is waiting for you," she croaked, before blowing her nose on a sleeve.

As if by magic, the fog that had enveloped us suddenly cleared up and there was Hel, in all her imposing monstrosity.

I know that's not a nice thing to say about a lady; however, Hel was truly monstrous. She had evil eyes in a face that was black and skeletal on one side, and normal on the other. On the normal side, she had long, straight black hair, while it was all gray and matted on the other side. Dressed in a long black robe, even the size of her was frightening. She was sitting on a throne and I barely came to her knees. Given her bulk, the throne was huge and it was made of human bones and skulls. A broom and a rake were leaning against the wall to the right of the throne. They, too, were huge, of course. I thought, what bizarre tools for a goddess, but Skap explained what they were for.

"Hel rarely leaves her residence, but when she does, she brings misfortune and illness. As she passes along the streets and through the villages, people suddenly get sick. If she sweeps the road with the rake, it means there will be survivors, but if she uses the broom, everyone will die."

Hel stared at us for a long time, while my knees went to jelly. I was even afraid to breathe.

"So, you did it, you managed to make it all the way here," she said, looking at me. Hel had a deep, evil sounding voice that made my blood curdle.

I barely managed to nod.

"Hey, are you deaf? I'm talking to you," she snarled.

"Yes, ma'am, I'm mean n-n-no, I'm not deaf."

"Would you care to tell me why you were so keen to come to my kingdom, or do I have to guess?"

"I have come to get something that was recently brought to you."

"What exactly? I receive numerous offerings every day and most of the time, I have no use for them."

"It's a necklace," I replied, vaguely.

"Necklace?"

"It's Brisingamen," said Skap, jumping in. Why does he always have to pick the wrong time to speak up? He would have made a rotten actor.

Hel skewered him, but only with her eyes. I didn't doubt she could do it for real, simply with a wave of her hand.

"This is really the last thing I would have expected. An elf that enters my realm and speaks to me with such disrespect. I wonder how he managed to cross the bridge. My faithful Modgud hates your type."

"We managed..."

"It was just luck," I told her, before Skap could say anything that would get us into even more trouble.

The goddess turned her evil eyes on me. I could see she was getting irritated because images of torture on the Nastrond beach appeared in her empty socket.

"Luck... Luck doesn't exist. The will of the gods rules the destiny of men," she screeched. "You say you have been lucky. But if now I decided to put an end to your life, would you still think you were lucky?"

I felt my stomach clench even tighter.

"No... That is, I was lucky in that moment," I replied.

"The usual reasoning of mere mortals."

"Well, actually...," I admitted.

"So, you came to get Brisingamen."

"Yes, I would like to get it back," I admitted.

She leaned forward. "You would like to take the only gift my father ever gave me?"

"I'm sorry, but Loki... Your father took it from the goddess Freyja, who would like to have it back."

"And she sent you to fetch it?"

"She would have liked to do it herself, but you know very well that you gods have rules that forbid her to visit you in your kingdom."

I saw her fumbling with the folds of her robe, until the necklace appeared in her hands. It must certainly have been very precious because it shone intensely, even in the dim light of that place. The necklace was a fine mesh made of a shiny metal, maybe silver, with a pendant representing a woman with a large necklace around her throat. The pendant gave off such brilliant flashes it seemed to have fire inside it.

"Here it is."

"That's her," exclaimed Skap.

"Why? You doubted, elf?"

"No, that is...," he started.

"It's just that we're happy to have found it," I stepped in.

"And now what do you want me to do, just give it to you?" she asked, mockingly.

"It would be very kind of you."

She burst out laughing in a way that made me shudder. It was a

117

mix of anger and malice. I felt that things were not going well.

"OK, then. I'll give it to you...," she cried.

Skap looked at me with a happy face. I couldn't believe my ears. I was going to thank her for the kind gesture when Hel added, "But then I will take your lives."

This time, I didn't want to believe what I heard. Had I really come to the end of my life? Yet, there had to be a way out.

"Here, young Heir. Hold in your hands the cause of your premature end," said Hel, exploding again into that awful laugh. She threw it at me and I grabbed it.

A strange thing happened: as soon as I touched it, I felt a little shove that made me raise my heels off the ground. It lasted only a moment, but I was sure I hadn't imagined it.

The necklace was nice and bright, but it certainly wasn't to die for! I held it in the palm of my right hand. When I moved it to the palm of my other hand, that feeling returned and this time lasted a few more seconds. I wondered if I had some invisible being behind me that was making fun of me.

As I moved it back and forth a few more times from one hand to the other, I realized that there was something about my left hand that, when it touched the necklace, caused a reaction.

Of course, it had to be the ring on my finger. The dwarves had forged both the necklace and the ring, so there must be some sort of strange alchemy between the two that caused the surprising reaction.

I brought them together again and the thrust made me hop forward.

I wondered what would happen if the contact lasted for a while. Could I fly?

I secretly hoped I had found a way to escape from that place. And Skap? I couldn't leave him there. But how could I take him with me?

"So, you like the necklace?" Hel asked me.

"Yes, it's very beautiful," I replied. "Skap, cling to me," I mumbled out of the corner of my mouth. The elf looked at me without understanding what I wanted.

"That's enough, now. Prepare to die."

"Skap, hug me, don't let me go," I urged a little more firmly.

"But, Aki... I don't think it's a good time to indulge in certain manifestations..."

"Do as I say."

Skap hugged me.

Hel laughed. "What a touching scene," she said, clapping briefly. She burst out laughing.

"Hold on tight and hope that it works."

"That what works?"

"You'll see."

I wrapped the necklace around the ring and formed a fist with my hand.

At first, it seemed that nothing was happening. Only a little forward hop, like the last sputter of a car that has run out of gas.

Come on, let's go, make me fly! I urged whatever sort of magic it was.

A more decisive jump, then I felt a powerful thrust that shot me straight up like a cannon ball.

"Nidhogg!" shouted Hel, after getting over the surprise.

We had played a nasty trick on the lady of the underworld and she certainly wasn't going to simply forget about it.

But we had made it.

We were flying!

I was afraid we were going to slam against the cave ceiling like bugs on a windshield. But somehow, we were flying through the sky. We sped through the chilly air, wrapped in the fog that prevented us from seeing where we were going. Our flight was totally out of control, but it didn't matter. We had just escaped certain death. I tried using my arms like wings so I could direct the course of our flight, but there was nothing doing. It seemed that we were being radio controlled from somewhere. In fact, a short time later we began to lose altitude as we started our descent to the ground. The impact with the ground was like falling from a height of six feet. It was a bit rough, but we didn't smash ourselves to pieces as I had feared. However, we had been flying pretty fast and we skidded on a patch of ice as we landed, like we were competing in the two-man bobsled at the Winter Olympics. We screamed like crazy as we slid along the ice, dodging shrubs and rocks. Our mad descent ended when we crashed into a mound of snow. We emerged completely shrouded in snow.

"Yay, we did it!" exulted Skap.

"Hold on before singing victory. Hel called Nidhogg, so we're not out of the woods yet."

My hair had frozen and it felt like I was wearing a helmet. It was so cold, I was struggling to close my eyelids. A flash announced the arrival of Gersemi.

"I'm so glad to see you guys," she said, and embraced us. "Did you get..."

"Here it is!" I exclaimed, showing her the necklace.

"But how did you...," but I didn't let her finish the sentence.

"Let's get out of here. I'm afraid it won't be long before Nidhogg hunts us down."

It took me a while to walk normally again because my knees had gone as stiff as two pieces of wood and they hurt like crazy.

However, seeing Nidhogg drove all the pain from my mind and I started to run.

FIFTEEN
ICE HORSES

"Run, run," urged Gersemi.

Easy for her to say. She glided along the icy ground like she was riding on a flying carpet. Furthermore, if things went wrong, she could always decide to disappear. Not to mention that her legs weren't frozen stiff like she had spent a night in the freezer.

Skap and I kept running, trying to stay upright on the frozen ground. It was like walking on a tightrope. When I looked back, I realized that Nidhogg was closing in on us. Before long he would be able to throw as many flames as he wanted at us.

By now I figured we must have been near the border to Hel's kingdom and that we would soon be crossing the Svartalfheim. That would mean getting trapped between Nidhogg hunting us from behind and the terrible Døkkalfar in front of us, with no way of escaping. But the landscape around us wasn't changing. We kept running through an ice forest, with fog that seemed to get heavier instead of lighter.

As Nidhogg caught up with us, he hurled a flame close enough to make me feel an intense heat that thawed me completely, like a croissant in the microwave.

"Over here," shouted Gersemi, leading us rapidly down a slope that took us into an impenetrable ice forest. The trees were so thick that it was impossible to see the sky above us.

We could hear Nidhogg's shrill cries. He was furious that we had managed to escape him.

"We got lucky again," panted Skap.

"But we can't stay here forever and I don't think that hellish dragon has any intention of leaving," I said.

In fact, a glow over our heads confirmed that the dragon was trying to melt the ice with his fiery breath.

"He'll never be able to do it," said Gersemi, without any doubt in her voice. "Here in Niflheim, nothing can defeat the ice."

"Niflheim? Another of the nine realms, right?" I asked.

"Yes, I thought we should take a different path back, given the welcome we got in Svartalfheim."

"That was a wise decision," I agreed.

Gersemi led the way through the ice forest, where we walked for ages along trails hidden by the tangle of ice-covered tree branches above us.

Nidhogg couldn't possibly follow us. And in fact, when the trail led us out of the ice forest, the horned dragon was nowhere to be seen.

I didn't dare even think about how angry Hel would be when she learned we were safe and sound. However, we shouldn't let our guard down yet. The goddess of the underworld had enough power that she could still hurt us.

"I think we're almost there!" exclaimed Gersemi.

"Where?" I asked.

"I told you about the goddess Skadi, right?"

"Yeah, sure, she's your teacher."

"I asked her to help us get out of Niflheim as quickly as possible. She is the goddess of frost and so...," she broke off. "Ah, here they are!" she exclaimed.

Three white horses came galloping towards us across the vast expanse of snow... But they were... They were made of ice!

"Let's go!" Gersemi urged us.

She jumped on one of the ice horses like an expert rider.

I mounted my horse, too.

Brrrrr...

Just imagine holding a giant ice cube between your legs and you'll know how I felt in that moment. Gersemi led our little group as we rode through the barren Niflheim tundra. We slowed down only once when Gersemi made us deviate from our route.

"Didn't you notice the footprint on the ground? Hrímthursar," Skap said, when I asked if he knew why we had gone in a different direction.

"Ice giants," I translated. As if fire giants weren't enough, I needed ice giants to complete my collection of amazing creatures encountered in the crystal of Yggdrasil.

However, we didn't actually run into any ice giants and we got out of Niflheim without further complications.

Except we hadn't considered that the ice horses would melt as soon as we left their kingdom. As a result, Skap and I ended up falling flat on our faces into in a muddy puddle, while Gersemi disappeared in a golden flash of blinding light.

But she returned in an instant, reappearing in the sky driving her mother's chariot.

"All board, we're going home," she cried out joyfully.

Destination: Asgard, the realm of the gods.

Gersemi drove the chariot recklessly, putting the cats through incredible moves in the sky. She let me have a turn driving and it was really exciting. I don't know how to describe the experience... It was awesome, that's for sure.

Suddenly, a glowing path appeared in front of us. Gersemi started down the trail, as sure of herself as if we had been on a highway in the sky. As we went down the trail, I noticed it was very colorful and I realized that we were traveling on a rainbow.

"It's the Bifrost bridge," explained Skap, who had noticed my look of surprise. "It's the only way to reach Asgard. Unless, of course, you'd like to wade across the rivers that you see down there, like the divine Thor is forced to do. He's forbidden from crossing the bridge because he would risk setting it on fire with the wheels of his powerful chariot."

Perched on a huge rock, Asgard appeared in the distance with such a bright glow that we were forced to look away. As we started going through the curtain of light, I suddenly felt better. It was like the fatigue I had accumulated over those last incredible few days had magically vanished.

The chariot descended rapidly and touched ground in front of a luxurious residence.

"Folkvangar!" exclaimed Skap.

"That's right, it's my mom's place," confirmed Gersemi.

The blinding white building had porticoes and colonnades, silver accessories, and terraces full of lush plants.

Frejya came to the stairway to welcome us. No longer angry with her daughter, she embraced Gersemi and then turned her attention to me.

I wondered how I looked after everything I had been through, and if I was decent enough to come before a goddess.

"Come, come along," she said, as if sensing my thoughts, and stretched her slender, manicured hands towards me.

I moved forward and she touched me softly on the cheek. I offered her the necklace that I was still clutching in my hand.

"Here, I have brought you Brisingamen."

"You have been clever and very brave," she said, gently taking it from my hands. "And you too, Skap," she added, making my elf friend gasp in surprise.

Now that the necklace was around Frejya's throat, it started glowing even brighter, like it had been charged with new energy.

"You are now free to follow the road that will take you back to the primary time world. However, I won't be the one to give you directions. The god you knew as a wanderer wants to meet you," she told me.

"Odin?" I exclaimed.

She nodded. "Go, he is waiting for you."

Before I could leave, Gersemi called out to me. "Aki, wait."

She came over and put her arms around my neck. I must have become red as a beetroot, because I could feel my face burning so much I was afraid my ears would end up grilled from the heat. I hugged her timidly with disgustingly slippery, clammy hands.

"I had fun and I really liked hanging out with you. And to think I had felt it was a punishment having to accompany you," she said, kissing me on the cheek.

I tried to reply, but I nearly choked on my own saliva.

"Thanks," I stammered. "I had a good time, too," I added.

"Have a great trip home," she said, then turned her back on me and hurried away.

As we left Folkvangar, Skap kept teasing me.

"You should have seen your face," he laughed. "Then you said... I h-h-had a g-g-good t-t-time, t-t-too," he doubled down.

"Go on, please go on jabbing at me," I said, thinking up millions of nasty things I could say to him.

"Oh, come on, follow me," he said, as we headed towards Odin's palace.

Walking through Asgard was like taking a stroll in an enchanted land. Avenues of fragrant flowers, trees full of fruit ripe for the picking, manicured lawns, deer and horses grazing in the fields, eagles and hawks flying in the clear sky, and streams flowing with clear, fresh water. Along the way, we also saw some luxurious houses.

One was made of gold, another had golden doors and a silver roof, but all of them were magnificent and splendid.

"There are twelve of them, one for each of the divinities that live in Asgard. Then there's Thor's house and the house that belongs to Frigg, Odin's wife," Skap explained.

We had come to a river that flowed through a plain where numerous warriors dueled and fought with each other. There were so many of them that I couldn't count them all. They wore helmets and armor, and were armed with lances, swords, shields and hammers. The clash of swords and armor, the blows of hammers on the shields, and the raucous cries of warriors echoing through the valley, contrasted with the peace and quiet of Asgard.

Just then, a glowing trail like a comet could be seen in the sky above the warriors, and the Valkyries, riding their magic steeds, appeared on the horizon.

Slowly they descended to the ground and rode along the plain until they reached the warriors. Three of them dismounted from their horses and grabbed hold of a man tied to a horse. They lifted him up and moved him like a puppet, so I figured he was dead, probably killed in battle.

They laid him on the ground and the eight Valkyries formed a circle around him. I saw one of them making signs with her hands while reciting obscure formulas, but I could only hear fragments of the words.

Then they remounted and trotted off towards a nearby magnificent palace that dominated over the plain.

The man slowly tried to raise himself. He sat up and looked

around bewildered, then he stood up and joined the other warriors who celebrated like he was an old friend whom they hadn't seen in ages.

"They're the einherjar, right?" I asked Skap.

"That's right, they're the brave warriors who died in battle. The army of the mighty Odin."

"And that building, the one where the Valkyries went inside?" I asked.

"Ah, that's the Frohheimr, Odin's palace. Inside is the great hall of Valhalla."

I had always thought of it as a special place, a kind of paradise for heroes. But the elf explained that Valhalla was like a huge room with five hundred and forty doors. It had walls made from the lances of the bravest warriors, a roof made of gold shields that depicted battle scenes, and benches covered in armor, while the interior furnishings were made from the garments worn by the warriors.

"Every day, the einherjar fight out on the plain, then in the evening they go inside Valhalla to feast and drink mead," concluded Skap.

"So that's where we have to go: Odin's palace," I said, pointing to the splendid building that glittered with gold flakes.

We crossed the river and entered the plain, accompanied by the raging warlike noises made by the mighty Vikings. Although they were only engaged in war exercises to keep the warriors in shape, they were really scary. It wouldn't take more than a glancing blow from one of the warriors to make my head roll.

We had almost reached Frohheimr's door when we saw a warrior with an ax running menacingly toward us. I was afraid it might have been an evil spirit sent by Hel, but he reached us before I even had time to think about running away.

"Young traveler," he said, and I immediately recognized him.

"Bjarni!" I exclaimed, relieved.

He picked me up like a feather, just as he had when we first met and I found myself again pedaling my feet in mid-air.

I had seen him with my own eyes when the Valkyries took him after he died in battle, yet he seemed alive and well, except for the glazed eyes that I found disturbing. At least the orbits weren't empty like those of the people who ended up with Hel.

"I heard about your mission. It takes a lot of courage to challenge the goddess of the underworld," he said as he put me back down.

"And a large dose of good luck, as well as the right friends. I'm still amazed that I managed to get out safely."

"Are you going back to the primary time world?" he wanted to know.

"Yes. I can't wait to get home."

Bjarni frowned. "I wish I could go back home, but now I have to stay here forever."

"But you are an einherjar, you are a warrior in the army of the most powerful of gods," protested Skap.

"You're right, but I lost a lot of things I very much cared about."

"For example?" Skap wanted to know, dissatisfied with the reply.

"My family," Bjarni answered, without hesitation.

Skap was about to speak, but then realized there was nothing he could say to that. For once he didn't say the wrong thing.

"Perhaps you can do me a favor. A great favor," Bjarni ventured.

"What?" I asked.

"I would like you to take a message to my son, Karli," he said.

We said we would and he gave us the message.

Believe me, I would never have imagined hearing such sensitive thoughts expressed through the mouth of a merciless warrior.

It was very touching.

SIXTEEN
SKAP'S BRAVERY

You want to know what Odin, the mighty god of the Vikings, looked like?

Let me tell you.

When we were taken in to see him, I thought I would find myself in front of a man who looked like the wanderer I had met on the bank of that stream. An elderly man with a wise expression, like that of a grandfather. And in a way, that's exactly what happened. But, to be truthful, only in a tiny way.

Just imagine Sean Connery with a bushier white beard, with long, white hair and a bandage over his right eye and you'll get a pretty good idea. Add to that, the expression of a man who has been around for thousands of years and has seen it all. Put that head and face on a Herculean type of body like... I don't know... Like, maybe the actor who played the Scorpion King, except the god was about nine feet tall. Now, imagine this guy brandishing his lance, Gungnir, and wearing a leather breastplate over a pair of brown trousers, held at the waist by a large belt with a gold buckle.

Well, I hope you get the idea of what Odin looked like.

"Mr. god... Mighty Odin..." I began, not sure how I was supposed to address him. "The divine Freyja said you were expecting me," I mumbled, keeping my eyes to the ground.

"What's the matter? You didn't look so scared during our first meeting," he said. "Is it because of the way I look?" he asked me and, before I could answer, he shrank down to the size of a normal man with the appearance of the drifter, including the hat and cane.

"The thing is, Mr. mighty god Odin, that day I didn't know who you really were."

"And am I very different?"

"Well, not right now... I mean yes, in the sense that you look like an elderly wanderer, except now I know who you really are."

"Maybe you prefer me like this?" he asked and changed again, taking on the guise of a pilgrim dressed as a prophet.

"It's not about the way you look..."

"I understand," he said, and changed back to his true appearance as the god of the Vikings.

"In all your transformations, your eye is always covered by a bandage and..."

"I sacrificed my eye so I could drink from the source of wisdom," he said dryly, as if he was surprised that I didn't know the reason for his mutilation.

"It's that at school they don't teach us to...," I tried to justify myself.

"I know, I know, spare me. I've heard troubling news that in the primary time world the gods are no longer important and that people's values are changing. That's not a good thing and I wonder if there's anything we can do to change it," Odin said, but I was pretty sure the question wasn't directed at me.

"I wouldn't know."

"You see, Knowledge helps you avoid unforgivable mistakes. Do you have any idea how dangerous your recklessness could have been?"

"Which recklessness?" The list was quite long.

"Ratatoskr. Having stopped him meant risking the destruction of our world. Certain balances should never be broken. Remember that."

"I will."

"But let's get to the reason why you're here. You need something from me, right?"

"Yes, I do."

"Listen."

He told me where to find the passage I had to go through to get back to Pieve Olimpia. Fortunately, Skap was with me, because I didn't know any of the places or landmarks Odin was telling me about.

"No problem. I'll take care of it," said Skap, with great confidence, but I didn't know whether to be happy or worried.

"Thank you for everything. Goodbye, mighty Odin," I said.

"Goodbye? It's difficult for an immortal god to understand the idea of goodbye. It sounds so final. I think 'see you later' is much better," he said.

He leaned forward to shake hands.

When he grabbed my hand, it almost disappeared in his much larger one.

We said goodbye to Frohheimr, and Odin let us borrow his horse to take us out of Asgard.

As I mentioned earlier, Sleipnir was a huge horse with eight legs. Not only he was unbeatable in a land race, he was also able to do other amazing things.

Asgard stood on a rock on top of a mountain, with slopes going down to the valley that were so steep as to be practically vertical. Well, Sleipnir walked down effortlessly, remaining glued to the rocky mountainside as if he had studded hooves. Skap and I had to hold on tightly to his mane to keep from flying off. As soon as his hooves touched firm ground, he picked up speed and raced off like a missile. Then he slowed down and came to an abrupt halt. Good thing I was clinging onto his neck, otherwise I would have taken an unforgettable tumble.

"Thanks, Sleipnir. Goodbye!" I said. In between the bzz bzz noises, I heard him say goodbye, too.

Skap set off without hesitation. Following Odin's directions, every time we came to a crossroad he never doubted which way to go.

I hoped for the best.

"Please, Skap, don't forget which way to go."

"I won't, don't worry. I'm not forgetting the promise we made to Bjarni. I'll take you to the passage, then I'll go immediately to his son," he promised solemnly.

"I wish I could have gone myself, but seeing you said we'd have to take a really long detour, I prefer to continue on this route."

"Of course, I understand your wish to go home."

"I sure do," I agreed.

I had lost count of the number of days I had been away from home. My watch was still stuck on the day and time when I had been catapulted into the crystal of Yggdrasil. I imagined the despair of my parents, and I wondered what Mr. Filippotti had told them. If he started talking about a Sphere of Time, parallel crystals and stuff like that, at the very least they would put him in a straitjacket and lock him up in an asylum. No one would ever have believed him.

However, I was sure that as soon as I was safely back home everything would be OK again. But I told myself that I would have to invent a plausible story, like "running away due to teenage problems." I couldn't tell the truth about my disappearance, unless

I wanted to spend the rest of my days talking to psychiatrists and taking medication to cure hallucinations.

That, however, was not my main concern at the moment. I hadn't seen Timoteo in ages and that was definitely my most alarming problem. Without my Gaia spirit, I wouldn't be able to get back home. Unfortunately, I had lost sight of him when he took off chasing after Ratatoskr, and I hadn't seen him since.

"Skap, what chance does an Heir have of returning to the primary time without the Gaia spirit?" I asked casually, like I was talking about the weather.

"Few... Maybe none," he blurted. Then he realized what he had said. "Sorry, I shouldn't have said that, should I?" he added.

"Let's just say that you were sincere and that you're not really great at reassuring people."

"I'm sorry."

"How far do we have to?"

"It's still a bit of a way. See that rock way over there?" he said, pointing to a dark spot on the horizon.

'Yes."

"It's a cave. According to Odin's directions, the passage is there."

"Well, let's hope that in the meantime Timoteo catches up to us," I said, even if there wasn't much time left. I would have to wait for him. I couldn't go back without him, because the risk of ending up in the middle of nowhere was too high.

"I hope so, too," agreed the elf.

A few minutes later our hope came to life. Timoteo was waiting for me in the middle of the path up ahead.

"Timoteo," I yelled, running up to him.

But Timoteo didn't move. He stood as still as a clay statue, like those they sell at plant nurseries.

Instead, it was the earth that moved. The path in front of us raised up to form a mound, then the soil slowly began to change shape, like clay being molded by invisible hands, until it took on the appearance of a man. But it was only a rough similarity.

"Loki," cried Skap, petrified with fear as he recognized the shape after the dust had settled.

After carelessly wiping the dirt off the shoulders of his yellow and black shirt, the god of chaos and great cunning looked at us. His crazy expression reminded me of the Joker in the Batman comic books.

Except his face was a dark greyish color and his eyes sent out yellow and red flashes, as if he had flames instead of pupils. He had a thin mustache and a goatee, both of them black like his shoulder length hair. He wore a leather helmet that looked like those worn by the early aviators. Like Odin, he was remarkably tall and his arms looked strong and muscular. He was holding Timoteo in the palm of his hand like it was a puppy. Unfortunately, the cat wasn't moving and I was afraid the god had killed him.

"Finally, I've found you!" he exclaimed.

"We didn't know you were looking for us," I said, without knowing where I had found the courage to speak. However, my legs were shaking.

"Oh, really? And did you think I wouldn't have minded when my daughter told me that you took the necklace I had given her?"

"The necklace belongs to the goddess Freyja and you stole it from her," I contradicted him.

"Blah blah blah... Because of that necklace, Freyja weeps gold tears and her husband has disappeared. I just wanted to do her a favor."

"It's not like that, and you know it."

"Where is Brisingamen now?"

"We returned it to the goddess."

"I'm too late, then."

"That's right, you can't do anything about it now," I challenged him.

"Hel's going to be upset, and unfortunately she has a really bad temper. I don't know what I'll have to come up with this time to calm her down. I'm afraid she will leave her throne and take the broom with her."

Skap gulped loudly. Hard times awaited the people of Midgard. The broom of the goddess of the underworld would claim many lives.

"What have you done to my cat?"

"Is this it?"

'Yes."

"I didn't know it was yours."

"I bet you did know," I snapped.

"You're touchy. Okay, okay, I knew. Do you want him back, by any chance?"

"Yes."

"And I want the necklace back. Now what?"

"There's nothing I can do about it, and anyway, the cat is dead," I said, fighting back tears.

"Looks like it is, doesn't it."

"What do you mean, it looks like it is?"

He touched the cat with a finger and Timoteo sat up as if he had just woken up.

"Timoteo," I cried, delighted.

He purred, happy to see me again. Now we had a big, humongous problem. Loki wouldn't let us go.

"Kitty, kitty," joked Loki and Timoteo began to hiss and growl as he flattened his ears. He looked like a miniature tiger.

"So, where's my necklace?"

"I told you the truth. We took it back to Freyja."

"Too bad, I guess I'll kill this beautiful furry kitty."

I was reading Timoteo's thoughts. He was about to do something and wanted me to run away really fast.

"Kitty, kitty," Loki continued. His nose was only a couple of inches away from the cat.

Timoteo took advantage of the situation. Baring his teeth and claws, he slammed into the face of the god who was taken totally by surprise. Skap and I took our chance to race off like Usain Bolt at the end of the hundred meters in the Olympics.

"Run, run," I urged Skap.

I quickly looked back and saw that Timoteo was keeping out of Loki's grasp. He jumped up and bounded to the ground. He began to run and soon caught up to us.

Loki didn't come after us. His terrifying laughter froze the blood in my veins as much as his words.

"Damn Heirs, I'm sure one of you stole my artifact Seidhr," he boomed.

I didn't know what he was talking about and anyway, I had nothing to do with it.

"What's he talking about?" I asked Skap, panting.

"About a powerful and dangerous artifact. Its nefarious magic can harm even at a distance," he said.

I didn't have time to ask him anything else.

"Fenrir," shouted Loki.

A tremendous howl filled the air and in the blink of an eye, a huge wolf came out of nowhere and began chasing us.

I remembered what Skap had told me about the fate of the Heir who had come to this crystal before me. I was afraid that history was about to repeat itself.

Fenrir was very fast and he kept getting closer by the second. Looking back, I caught only a glimpse of him, but that was enough to scare me.

He was as big as an elephant and had really sharp fangs.

We were almost at the entrance to the cave, but Fenrir would be on us before we had time to reach it.

"Go, I'll take care of him," yelled Skap.

"No, he'll kill you."

"What happened before must never happen again," he said and stopped running.

I watched as Skap took his bow and attached an arrow to it. It was a perfect shot that centered the wolf's nose, making him slow down and move more carefully.

As I entered the cave, I saw Skap flee in a different direction.

It was dark in the cave and I didn't know what to look for. But Timoteo did.

I followed him as we passed through increasingly narrow recesses until we reached a nook not much bigger than a washing machine.

"I have to go in there?" I asked Timoteo, who replied that I did.

As I bent down, my eye caught a metal object covered in dirt.

I picked it up.

It looked like a coin, but there wasn't enough light to tell for sure. I put it in my pocket.

It took quite a bit of work, but I finally got into the crevice.

I sat cross-legged and Timoteo sat in my lap. I put my hands on two rock ledges that looked like the gearshift of a car, and I waited. At first nothing happened, then suddenly I felt an intense heat in my palms that slowly spread throughout my body.

As I was thinking of Skap, hoping he had been able to get to safety, the darkness surrounding me dissolved into a ball of light and everything began to spin.

I closed my eyes.

SEVENTEEN
TIME STANDS STILL

When I opened my eyes, my hands were resting on the Sphere of Time and Mr. Filippotti was with me. I had made it!

I was back in Pieve Olimpia. I breathed a huge sigh of relief as Timoteo jumped down from my shoulder and walked away.

"We have to go to my place, they'll be concerned," was the first thing I said.

"Hold on, don't run," Mr. Filippotti blocked me. "There's no rush."

"What do you mean, there's no rush? I've been gone for days. Everyone will be worrying about me."

"Actually, the primary time hasn't moved very much since you left."

"What do you mean?"

"What time is it?" he asked me.

"My watch is broken. It must have happened during the transfer."

"Look at it."

The second hand had never stopped moving and... The day was the same but the time... The time had changed. Two hours and three minutes ahead of where my watch had first stopped.

"See?"

"I don't understand."

"In the crystals, time keeps turning over on itself. How can I explain it... Let's see. When you're in a crystal, you have the impression that time passes in the same way as in the primary time world and, in a way, it does. However, when you crossed back through the doorway to the primary time world, the amount of time that went by on the crystal is compressed into a much shorter period."

"It means that I have been away for... I dunno, five or six days, but here it was only two hours?" I asked in disbelief.

"Yes, exactly. The passing of time seems identical but the transfer compresses it. Basically, it ends up working out just like you said."

"So... So, my mom is still here in your house," I said with relief.
Mr. Filippotti nodded." But now we'd better go back upstairs. Otherwise, she'll soon come looking for us."

I felt better, much better.

"So, how was your trip?"

"A whole lot of totally crazy stuff happened... Odin, Loki, Thor, Hel...," I began, as we climbed the stairs.

"You went into the crystal of Yggdrasil, right?"

"So you knew!"

"No, I didn't know where the Sphere of Time would take you. I could tell from the names you just mentioned. They're the gods of the Vikings who live in the crystal of Yggdrasil."

"I discovered a lot of things, but you already know most of them and you didn't tell me anything, my dear Master of Knowledge," I scolded. "Even Brokk and Eitri, two very wise dwarfs, criticized you for not teaching me anything."

"There was no time to tell you because I wasn't sure if you were truly an Heir, but I'll make it up to you," he said, as we walked into his study.

"Among other things, they told me that there are seven spheres!" I exclaimed.

"That's true," he confirmed.

Then he took a dusty map out of a cabinet. He unrolled it on the table.

It was a map of Europe and part of Asia. I looked at it.

Some of the regions of Italy still appeared as possessions of the Byzantine Empire. "Here, see... No, this one is too old," he said.

He took out another map. This one was more recent, although New York still appeared as New Amsterdam.

"This one isn't any good either."

"It must be this one," he huffed, as he unrolled yet another map.

"As I said, there are seven spheres and their locations are circled in red."

"But here you can only see six, because the seventh one is constantly on the move."

"Right. The seventh one is a roving sphere and it's impossible to

know exactly where it is right now. "

Amazing to think that one of the spheres was in my home town. Pieve Olimpia was only a village. The other spheres were in obscure locations around Europe and the Middle East. Maybe they were small towns or villages like mine. None of the spheres was in a major city like Rome, London or Berlin.

"Come on now, tell me about your trip," Mr. Filippotti urged me.

I began to tell him about all the things that had happened, but I knew it would take hours. As I was speaking, I started to wonder if I hadn't gone crazy and just dreamed the whole thing.

Was it really possible that I had been transported to another world?

Had I really talked with the gods of Asgard?

Had I really escaped from the jaws of Fenrir and the Nidhogg's flames?

Honestly, I struggled to believe the things I was saying. Yet I really had lived through it all. Or maybe not.

My mom knocked on the door. She cracked it open. "Mr. Filippotti, I'm done."

I was so happy to see my mom again that I wanted to throw my arms around her neck and hug her.

"Achille, I hope you've been behaving and didn't make a nuisance of yourself."

So much for that, the warm and fuzzy moment was over. Thanks, Mom!

"No trouble at all, far from it. Your son is a smart, lively kid and if he wants to come visit me again, I'd be happy to see him."

"Thanks! Come on, let's go."

"OK. See you soon, Mr. Filippotti. I can't wait to hear more stories," I said.

He winked at me. I had stories to tell him, too.

I went out in the yard. Timoteo was lying on the hood of my mom's car, waiting for me.

"Hey, buddy," I said, stroking him. He replied with a large dose of purring.

"You were a great traveling companion."

He told me that I was, too. Even cats know how to lie. On the way home, I wondered if my parents knew that I was an Heir. Was it possible that I had inherited it from one of them? Who knows.

I tossed around a couple words in Old Norse, but my mom looked at me like she had caught me with a finger up my nose. No, she probably wasn't an Heir, unless she had other powers that I couldn't imagine.

When we got home I ran up to my room. Everything was exactly as I had left it. After all, I had only been gone a few hours.

The more I thought about it, the more it all seemed totally unreal. I'd talked with Odin...

If I shared that with anyone, at the very least they would think I was crazy. Then I'd end up as a "case study" in a psychiatric magazine, with a nice photo to go along with the article.

But it really had happened.

I lay on the bed with my hands under my head.

When I closed my eyes, many of the things that had happened flashed through my mind.

The fire giants and the trolls.

Freyja and the chariot drawn by cats.

The Valkyries.

Gersemi...

I had seen so many things, but I couldn't tell anyone about them; that is, not counting Mr. Filippotti, who had undoubtedly seen and heard a lot more than I had.

And what if somehow he had made me have hallucinations?

Maybe he was a psycho and...

I remembered the coin. I took it out of my pocket and was amazed by what I saw.

It was a Peruvian coin: a Nuevo Sol coined in 2010.

But that was impossible!

What did a 2010 Peruvian coin have to do with the crystal of Yggdrasil?

It didn't make any sense.

"Aki, are you in your room?"

It was my sister.

I hid the coin under the sheets.

"Yes, I'm here."

Aurora came in.

"Why are you sleeping?"

"I'm not sleeping."

"But you're in bed."

"I'm not sleeping."

"I had fun with daddy today," she said, throwing herself at me. We wrestled and I tickled her. I liked to hear her laugh.

"What about you? What did you do with mom?"

"Nothing special. I got bored," I lied shamelessly.

"What's that?"

"What?"

"That ring."

"Oh, nothing," I lied, hoping she didn't want to see it up close. I quickly slipped it off and put it away in a drawer. It still had the runic inscriptions on it.

So I hadn't imagined the whole thing. I wasn't crazy.

It really had happened.

Hey guys, how cool is that!

ACKNOWLEDGEMENTS

I want to thank the small contingent of young explorers who first traveled through the parallel crystals, Martina, Jacopo, Alberto, Mattia and Stefano, all students and alumni of the A. Ronchetti Middle School in Pogliano Milanese, for reading the manuscript and giving me valuable suggestions.

Thanks also to Cristina Giussani, an Italian teacher, for her time and collaboration.

I also want to express my gratitude to the awesome illustrator, Luca Rovelli, for agreeing to work his magic in bringing to life the characters of the crystals.

Finally, I wish to thank Laura Colombo for her continued enthusiasm and support.

Finito di stampare nel mese di Aprile 2016
per conto di Youcanprint *Self-Publishing*

Made in the USA
Middletown, DE
12 December 2022

18143141R00087